T0064457

SAPTAPADI

SAPTAPADI

Seven Steps to Freedom

BOBBY PATNAIK

PARTRIDGE
A Penguin Random House Company

To order additional copies of this book, contact
Partridge India
000 800 10062 62
orders.india@partridgepublishing.com

www.partridgepublishing.com/india

CONTENTS

Dedicated to Baba & Mom

Not possible without the love and support of
Mummy, Daddy
and, most of all,
Ravi

For Pranav and Pranshu

THE RELUCTANT TRAVELLER

Sujata did not like to travel. It was as simple as that. It was not so much the strain of packing and preparing – in fact that was the part she enjoyed. Deciding what to wear on which day, whether the yellow sari would serve the formal occasions on one of the evenings more or the handloom cotton one she bought from *Boyanika*. Accessories – colour coordinated to each outfit, the black metal *jhumkas* for the dressy salwar kameez, the chunky gold-plated one for the cotton sari and the faux stones for the Western suit. Shoes were a perennial problem; while the flat ones suited the day long rigour of running around, for the evening while she would have wanted to wear something stylish, her old back problem would not allow her to. Nighties, – the good peach-colored one she kept for special occasions – underclothes, hairdryer, cosmetics, her favourite paperback stuffed into the top pocket of the strolley for easy retrieval, it was actually fun. But it was the preparation that she had to do at home to manage things in her absence that made it stressful. The cook had to be told the menu well in advance, and even then he would call at all points of time, bang in the middle of a meeting, to ask whether it was *arhar* dal that day or *chana*. The other maid for the *jhadoo pochha* had to be warned not to take off on any day during her absence. The kids' project homework had to be completed before she left, or they would not do it after her. Pradeep was another problem, inspite of her telling him to be back home early every day, he would forget and then she would have to call him and remind.

At office also she had to ensure no major files were pending, else the boss would not let the occasion pass for a snide remark on how people were more intent on travelling than managing their regions well. But that was still a manageable thing. It was a nice, cushy job. The work was long but not too arduous. She had joined the bank in the early days and the benefits of growth in business had come to those who had joined the firm during its starting days. Promotions had come early and for those who were eligible and completed the requisite qualifications, it had been a time-based one.

It was the home front that was irritating and frequently she ended up with more frayed nerves before travelling. Hence any impending need to travel was a potential stressor.

Earlier it used to be worse. The kids were small. She had to travel for an hour every day, each way. Every day used to be like a mini travel, starting with early morning chores – the kids' breakfast, tiffin, getting them ready for school, Pradeep's early morning tea, instructions to the cook for lunch, get ready and run to the bus stop. Every day, five days a week. Weekends used to be preparatory time for the week day rush. No, she did not welcome at all, the idea of more strain brought on by a travel.

But unknown to her, slowly the hour spent on bus travel, to and fro, started to become 'her' time. One hour she could spend on day dreaming – on how life could have been different had she taken up the lecturership offer in her home town instead of the glamorous-seeming bank job, what if she had not refused the promotion offer of regional head of a neighouring country, what if she had married someone else, what to wear tomorrow, what to cook for dinner – somehow there never seemed to be a dearth of things to ruminate on. She started to look forward to the journeys. The whole morning in between egging the kids, waking the husband and directing the cook the impending journey lingered pleasantly on her mind, like a pleasure waiting to be savoured. And in the office, in the middle of meetings, calls, files that had to be disposed off immediately, head office calling on some settlement gone wrong, the thought of the journey back gave her sustenance to bear the mundaneness of her normal life. Her thoughts were not only of her – she thought of faraway gardens, unexplored mountains, galaxies that mankind would never see, thoughts that may never cross anyone's mind – the whole universe and those beyond were her mind's playground.

And then she started getting directives to travel, to other cities, as part of her senior role in the bank. Though she had passed up the opportunity to head a bigger area in another country, she had still moved up the ladder to handle a bigger region and was responsible for other cities in the south zone. Initially she looked for all excuses possible to avoid the travel. The kids used to be an easy one earlier, now however with both having grown up, that did not hold good. She did not have parents or parents-in-laws staying with her and so elderly-ill health was not a valid reason. Her boss knew Pradeep had a city-bound job so she could not give the excuse of kids being alone at home without parents. 'It comes with the job' was also the refrain from Pradeep whenever she cribbed about the travel.

At first, the very thought of staying away from the kids for days together irritated her. However she started seeing that they actually managed fine on their own. Both had been brought up to be independent – she had taught them to do their own work themselves without depending on anyone – and that helped when she was away. When she started her travels, she would call up at least thrice a day to check whether they had gone to school on time, eaten their tiffin, done their homework etc. However she slowly stopped doing it when she saw her frequent calls were actually irritating them instead of helping. The cook is whom she had to call multiple times because no matter how detailed her instructions, he managed to botch up a couple of dishes, Pradeep would be certain to allude to it when she called in the night for a summary of the day. However an interesting thing happened as a fallout – Pradeep started to get interested in cooking. Of course half the credit for that went to the new only-food channel launch on television recently – starting from Sanjeev Kapoor to Nigella Lawson, all were frequent visitors to their living room now. Invariably when she called in the evening, Pradeep would be in the kitchen trying his hand at some new kind of pasta or *handi paneer* with the cook complaining to her about the messy kitchen he left behind. But whether over time Pradeep got better with his culinary skills or the cook simply welcomed the work taken off him, the outcome was, many-a-time when she called in the evening, the cook would be watching television, Pradeep pottering in the kitchen and girls happily giggling over Papa's last night's special from *Highway on my Plate.* What she felt was a combination of a twinge of envy and regret that she was not missed much along with a sense of relief that all was well. The relief was what made her relax and that's when she started enjoying the me-time of her travels.

When the flight took off, it felt almost like a physical lifting off from the ties that bound her down. For the next one to two hours it was like a transition, a suspension in a state of non-beingness, a lightness of being. Being twenty thousand feet above ground was like being twenty thousand feet above worldly cares. She took pleasure in thumbing through the in-flight shopping booklet which in any case by her third travel she knew by heart. Her dislike of the cold sandwiches did not decrease, but with time even the economy airline she travelled on started to introduce ready-to-eat hot alternatives which though almost meagre in amount still were much better than the other option. She loved the ritual of making coffee on the flight – open the tray table, tear open the small pouch of dairy whitener and the sugar-free into the small white plastic cup, stir in the coffee with the cute stirrer provided and sip the otherwise watery coffee which she hated, with a strange sense of contentment. She was tempted to buy some of the obnoxiously priced in-flight products on the booklet but stopped short of that one – some lunatic had priced them obviously. Watching the co-passengers leaf through the latest paperbacks, haggle with the air hostess on why some thing was not available on the menu, squeeze their way to the rest room, and snore while trying to keep their heads from rolling off was also something she enjoyed with a newly found voyeur's pleasure. She even liked the mechanical, plasticky smile and 'Thank You' from the airhostesses on the way out – it was like a secret message gesturing to her alone that they knew she liked doing this and was looking forward to the next one.

She did not like the disembarking part though, it was like coming back to *terra firma*. But once she was in the cab bound for the hotel, the sights and sounds of a new city enraptured her. So many possibilities opened up before her, possibilities that she knew she never would try, but nevertheless the simple fact of the possibility being there was tantalizing.

The first thing she did on reaching the hotel was to fling the bags and sink into the six-inch mattressed bed. She loved the white sheeted, head boarded beds in the hotel. Many of her friends used to crib that after a few travels they hated the very sight of a hotel room, she wondered why it never happened with her. The luxurious bathroom with the sunken tub, the huge TV, the small refrigerator stocked with cold drinks and sometimes even an occasional liquor bottle, the velvety drapes which when you drew aside you could see the oval pool with its sparkling blue water, the dim lights, the courteous staff, she never ever got tired of these small luxuries. It was undiluted contentment to lie in bed till late morning without anyone asking where the maths book was or what needed to be cooked for lunch. To call for morning-tea which came in one of those lovely floral-patterned teapots, to be able to dawdle in the bathtub with

Saptapadi

the morning newspaper. She wore her best silks and cottons on trips, it somehow made sense to dress well when she felt so good about everything. The day would pass off in a haze of meetings in the local office of the bank. Coming back to the hotel in the evening felt like homecoming. Sometimes she would go to the nearest market instead of coming to the hotel. It was fun to potter in the shops, checking *saris*, makeup articles, shoes – she got all these in the city she lived in, in fact more because her trips were generally to smaller cities which she managed by remote, but it never felt so good to shop there. Most of the times, she actually did not buy anything but just sat in a coffee shop over a steaming large cup of cappuchino, observing the comings and goings. In the evening when she reached her room, the housekeeping would have kept the mandatory rose and two toffees by her pillow with a 'good night' message. She felt pampered to say the least.

It was on one such trip that she met Roshan. He was staying in the same hotel as she was. That day there was a throng of tourists at the hotel and by the time she reached the breakfast room, all tables were full. She had to sit at the only place available. A gentleman was already sitting there, sipping what seemed to be a post breakfast coffee and looking at the newspaper. He looked up briefly when she sat down and said 'hi' before returning back to his paper. Had it not been for the maitre'd, their interaction would have been probably restricted to that brief word. However he came with a request. 'Madam, you had booked a cab for Gate Road. However there are no cabs available today as most of them have been booked for site seeing trips by the tourists

7

who arrived yesterday. However Sir has a cab which is going to Gate Road' he gestured towards the gentleman at the table. 'If you could share it with him…' he left the sentence trailing. 'We will work it out' the gentleman replied to him dismissing him off. And that's how they started talking.

He worked as an auditor for an investment bank, and frequently had to travel to the city they were in, for regular auditing exercises. As they travelled in the cab to the same area, he to his bank and she to hers, they spoke about work, families and life in general. On the outside he had seemed the quintessential auditor – quiet, even a little crotchety, complete with horn-rimmed glasses, plain suit and a briefcase. As they talked however, he seemed affable, laughing easily, cracking jokes, being self-deprecating without being self conscious. Despite herself she started comparing him with Pradeep – by any standards Pradeep was a good husband, but being easy never came naturally to him. At most parties he would be tongue-tied, preferring to hang around with his own set of friends. He never liked jokes about himself taking it as some sort of an affront if she cracked an innocuous one on him. She tried to stop herself, it was not fair on Pradeep. She knew he loved her with that quiet steadfastness that was like him. In any case this was not even remotely about love. Somehow the fact that she found Roshan so easy to be with jelled with the rest of feel-good she had associated with trips.

They met again in the evening, since she did not have a hotel cab and planned to take an autorickshaw back, he offered to pick her as he said he would finish work mostly around the same time. On the way back, he asked her if she planned to go back straight to the hotel. 'I was planning to catch a movie and dinner outside by myself, but if you are interested…' he left the sentence unfinished. She had never done this, with colleagues she had gone out multiple times, but never with a rank stranger. But his eyes were completely innocent, devoid of any other hidden message if someone tried to find it. 'I have nothing better to do, so yes why not' she took a leap of faith.

The movie was tolerably average, thankfully it did not have any scenes that would have made her cringe to watch with him. He had chosen carefully, she felt relieved about that. Dinner however made up for the movie, it was delectable fare, and they ate slowly, leisurely, talking all the time. They spoke about movies they liked, books they had read – he read serious stuff as opposed to her bestseller paperbacks and he joked about it, but in a way that did not make her feel bad – about kids, and about spouses. He spoke with genuine affection about his wife, and she loved that, she never trusted men who criticized their spouses. On the way back however, somehow the conversation became more about them. Their personal likes and dislikes, thoughts, dreams, and she found herself sharing some of her innermost fears and desires with him. He listened quietly and intently, never once interrupting her, smiling when she said something funny. After some time they both fell into a silence but it was not one of those awkward silences, it was a warm, companionable silence, the kind you have with an old friend. He broke it as the cab neared the hotel.

'I am flying back tomorrow morning'.

'Oh is that so?' Suddenly she felt the warmth dissipating. 'I leave the day after'.

'When will you visit next…'

'Can't say but as regional manager for this region I have to visit intermittently. Maybe I can make my visits quarterly…' the second sentence had come out without her intending to say it at all.

'Monthly not possible?' he left the question hanging in mid-air.

'I can certainly try…'

'This is my card' he said fishing out a visiting card from an ivory coloured box. 'Drop me a note on my mail id when you plan to visit, I have the liberty to plan my visits'.

She took the card and kept it in her fist. They departed in the lounge wishing each other good night. In her room, Sujata dropped on her bed and closed her eyes. In movies a meeting like this is supposed to leave both protagonists with a sense of incompleteness and longing, she however felt only a strange sense of lassitude spreading over her. 'We will only meet and spend an evening like this obviously there's nothing more to it' she told herself, but she could not stop the delightful feeling of possibilities which may or may not become realities.

The next day was a hectic day in office. Intermittently the thought of Roshan's flying back that day came to her, and she did think once of calling him, but she stopped herself. There was no reason to call, besides he had been very specific that the only way of connecting was on the mail address.

She came back late in the night and dropped off to sleep without even packing for the next day's travel back. It was an early morning flight and it was thankfully the hotel's wake-up call that awoke her in time. With alarm she saw she was going to be late unless she really rushed. She just had time to brush her teeth and stuff her belongings into the strolley before rushing out. All throughout the way the cab driver kept on remonstrating with her that he had to drive fast amidst traffic because she had started late. She was too tense to even reply to him. She almost threw the money at the cabbie and ran for check-in. 'Madam, we have been announcing your name, where have you been?' the lady at the counter was almost indignant. Somehow she checked her luggage and finished security check and ran to the air craft which was just fifteen minutes away from taking off. The air hostesses did their own share of glaring at her, but all she cared to do then was stow her handbag in the overhead cabin and sink into her seat. After the plane took off, she loosened her seat belt and inclined her seat. The morning rush and early wake-up had been too much, before she knew she fell into a deep sleep. She woke up when the airhostess came and nudged her with 'Madam, we are about to land, please straighten your seat and fasten your seat belt'. She had slept through the snack and beverages break, her favourite in-flight entertainment. 'Anything for a hot cup of coffee' she thought to herself; anyway she would be home soon.

At the airport Pradeep and the kids were there to pick her. She felt a sense of guilt on seeing Pradeep, as if she had been doing something wrong. Quietly she chastised herself, you have just had a dinner and movie with someone, chill down, she told herself. But somewhere inside a small voice asked 'and what about trying to make monthly visits now'.

They reached home and she asked the cook to make a cup of coffee first. The kids started rummaging in her bags for goodies that she generally brought from her trips.

'Hey, there is a piece of good news' Pradeep started 'I met Kumar yesterday at the pub'. Kumar was her boss and he and Pradeep shared a bonding that men could have only when they have had a drink together, even if once. This bonding did nothing to better Kumar's bossiness towards her, it was as if Pradeep was someone else and he had two separate relationships with two different people.

'Ok, and what did he say' she asked trying to help the elder one find a chocolate. Thanks to her evening spent in movie and dinner with Roshan, she had not managed to pick anything other than chocolates for the kids this time. The next day she had come back too late to shop. They were going to be disappointed.

'My dear, you have been promoted' Pradeep smiled. 'You are now promoted to the position of General Manager' Pradeep was genuinely happy for her. 'And what's more is, you don't have to do what you hate so much – travelling. The regional managers who will report to you will do all the leg work'.

'Oh' she said looking at him blankly.

'What? I give you such good news and all you can say is oh!' there was surprise on Pradeep's face

'Not it's just that I was not expecting this now…'

'Yeah that's what Kumar said, and he said that this would come as such a pleasant surprise to you. Anyway I am off to the club, will be back in a couple of hours' Pradeep gave her a quick peck and left the room.

'I must inform Rosan immediately on this' she thought and started rummaging for his card in her purse feverishly. It was not there. 'I must have dropped it into the strolley' she thought and just as she was about to search in there, she remembered. She had been holding it in her fist when she dropped off to sleep. The next day she left for office and came back late, and woke up late for her flight. That's when she had stuffed her things into the strolley without remembering that she had dropped the card on the bed a couple of nights earlier. The card would be still on the bed, if housekeeping had not swept it away while cleaning the room.

'Ma, what should I cook for lunch' the cook had come in with her cup of coffee.

Window Shopping

Latha was known as a good cook, she prided herself on being one. A dish gone wrong was like a heresy for her. And hence Vijayan was so surprised at her lack of reaction when he told her the *poha* was salty, at breakfast table. On her part, Latha thought, he is looking at me as though I have killed a cow. Muttering 'I don't know what's wrong with you nowadays' Vijayan left his *poha* untouched and got up from the table and began putting on his shoes. Normally Latha would have been mortified that he was going to office without breakfast. Her whole life revolved around feeding. Feeding him, feeding the kids, even feeding the neighbours. Today however she was too distracted to feel anything. Mechanically she lifted the plate, emptied the contents into the dustbin and kept the plate in the sink. Vijayan was utterly surprised. Generally she would rush around, trying to offer alternatives to him should he find the breakfast not good. If for some reason he was not feeling well and did not eat breakfast, she would call him up umpteen times in the office to ask if he had something, drank tea till he got irritated. Today there was no call at all. 'I think she is menopausal' he thought.

Latha put the *dal* in the cooker to make *sambar* and lay down on the bed thinking of the black strapless dress she had seen yesterday. Usually she would not see such stuff on

Mall Road where they shopped. Vijayan was a lower level clerk in a small private office in the quaint South Indian town they lived in. With two kids in school, and in-laws back in the village to send money to, there was no way they could afford to shop anywhere other than Mall Road. The more upmarket Southside bazaar was for the upper class and it is there that such dresses were available, she had seen once when they had gone on a sight-seeing trip around the city. But then there were so many other things available there. Eyeliners that gave you a heavy lidded look like in movies, glossy lipsticks six inches long, funky bags and chic looking purses, and dresses galore like the black one she had seen yesterday in Mall Road. More than the wares in the shops though, she wanted to stare at the women walking in Southside bazaar. They were dressed in *saris,* trousers, *salwar kameezes*, long frocks, but no matter what they wore, they smelt of class. She was sure it was class and not just money. She had seen one of Vijayan's colleagues come into money suddenly, his foster grandfather died unexpectedly leaving him a lot of money. But nothing changed. Except that instead of cotton cushion covers and bed sheets they started using some horrible maroonish brocade material that looked cheap and tacky. In fact, he changed all furnishings to maroon and repainted the entire house pinkish – like a diluted poor cousin of maroon; along with money he had also acquired a weird understanding of what magazines called colour coordination. No, she could smell class, and had she not been unfortunate to be born and married into a lower middle class family she would have smelt the same. She knew it, it was not some delusion she carried out of ego, it was something she had known all along since her teens.

She was much more sophisticated inside than any of the women in the colony for lower level clerks that she lived in. Even when she dressed for a marriage reception or a birthday party, the women would ask her why she did not wear a *Banarasi*. To them the simple light blue cotton *sari*, starched and ironed, with a sleeveless deep blue blouse, made no sense at all. They would be dressed in oranges, reds, blues, replete with golden borders, their best gold jewellery in display. By contrast she would have a simple pair of studs that was fake but looked classy and two light bangles on her hand. Earlier they used to ask; after a couple of social events, the gossip spread. They would gather together like a bunch of hens and speak quietly, and she had no doubt that much of it was to do with her sense of dressing. Even Vijayan would look askance at her as they would be about to leave for a ceremony, not daring to ask however why she did not dress like others, because somewhere he knew that she was a cut above the mediocrity he was steeped into. She knew that.

When she was a schoolgirl, she thought she would study hard and gather enough momentum to shoot out of the orbit of middle classness that she was born into. Something like the escape velocity they taught in the physics class. But try though she might, her results always felt short of that magical benchmark which would have catapulted her into the arena of the rich and famous. She could not clear any of the entrance exams to professional courses, her marks were just okay to get her admitted to an Arts course in college. Stubbornly she refused to take up Home Science, which her mother thought would make her marriage worthy, she hated the giggling girls in the Home Science room full of pots and pans. 'Are you going to become a Prime Minister with that Political Science subject of yours?' her mother would grumble. But she refused to give in.

Secretly she harboured another fond dream. That someone with money and class would take a strong liking to her, attracted to her innate sophistication beneath the façade of mediocrity and that would be the beginning of her entry into the ethereal world of soft lights, velvety furnishings, crepe cottons, imported lipsticks in subtle colours and those long gowns. There again she missed the bus, she was not bad looking, but there was nothing outstanding in her features. Probably if she had been born to a better economic strata, she would have looked different, but she wasn't and so she melted with the other girls into the background. All through her life she watched men get fascinated with girls who were good looking in a sort of over the top way, with she, certainly more eligible, watching helplessly from the sidelines as fate overtook her. When the proposal came from Vijayan's family, she quietly acquiesced, not seeing any reason to think her life would get any better.

To be fair though, immediately after marriage, she had got her hopes up. In the first flush of marriage, when even the most mundane of surroundings took on a rosy hue, she acquired a fresh train of thoughts. She would work on Vijayan and he would be her ticket to freedom from the ordinary. He had the calibre, he was hardworking, that was all that was needed to get onto something better. He could become a fast-tracker and get his promotions earlier than the rest and in no time would be an officer. While that did not come close to the slightly stratospheric realms she aspired to, it was the first rung of the ladder. Even better, with a little luck, he could even get a great offer and join in a larger enterprise in a senior role. Things could get only better from thereon. Initially Vijayan went along with her gentle nudges to work harder, apply for another qualification on the side, keep the boss happy and even look out for positions in the *Times of India Ascent* on Wednesdays. He would indulge her fantasies of a very different life than what they lived. However slowly she saw him starting to get irritated with even implicit suggestions for bettering himself. With her exhortations he had started to work till late in the office, now however he started reverting to his original schedule of returning by five in the evening. The red encirclings on *Ascent* began to fade, and all grand plans to enroll in an evening course that would add to his biodata, disappeared. Sad, she realized that he was never made for grander things, he did not have a desire to, in the first place, he was a simple man who preferred the welcome routine of everyday life. She left off pushing him, and perceptibly enough, he relaxed, settling back into his old groove.

She had been married for eight years. Now she was convinced that nothing much was going to change for her. But even then like a sleeping hydra, sometimes the desire to break free from the eight hundred square feet house that she called home, rose fierce and raging within her. Such a moment was what she was undergoing now, after she saw the black strapless dress in Mall Road yesterday.

She had almost missed it. The shop was a new one and not in her usual path within the marketplace. However her daughter needed some coloured beads for a school project and not finding it anywhere, she had ventured into one of the narrow alleys which is where she saw the dress from the glass window. Her first reaction was of utter surprise, Mall Road did not stock such things. Then she saw it, it was a small boutique, wedged between a wholesale shop of cotton bed sheets and an electronics shop. Easy to miss any day. The dress hung on the mannequin, seamless, the folds perfect, the black not the shimmery one of cheap material but a dull, soft black, the material clinging to the curves of the inanimate figure. It would look much better on her, unlike most of the women in the colony she had not let her figure go after child birth. Surreptitiously everyday she would touch her toes at least twenty times in the bathroom. Studiously she avoided the fried snacks she made for Vijayan, leading him to once pass a snide remark 'what are you so figure-conscious about, you planning to marry again' the typical kind of down market comment she hated. So while the other women carried post-delivery bulges, her stomach was as flat as it was when she was just a girl. Her shoulders would show up rounded – they were neither bony nor too fleshy – and she had a good torso. The ache to possess the dress became almost physical. But how. Almost each rupee in Vijayan's monthly pay packet was accounted for. Monthly rent, groceries, school fees, vegetables and milk took up the lion's share of the salary. Next came insurance payments, sundry bills, Vijayan's monthly commuting expenses, medical bills that had a habit of popping up in the most stringent of months, some ceremony or a marriage back in the village. It hardly left enough to save a decent amount every month. At times she felt suffocated at the inability to indulge even the minutest of desires.

The price tag on the dress read two thousand rupees. That was still much less than what it would have cost at Southside, there it would not have been anything less than almost double the amount. She wondered how the price wasn't as much. The fabric seemed okay though. After a lot of inner struggle she gingerly stepped inside the shop. It was a small shop but welcoming and cosy. The salesman also seemed most unlike the Mall Road rowdies who decided that if you had entered their shop you would not leave without buying at least a handkerchief. He was courteous and gentlemanly, and most non-intrusive as she fingered the fabric lovingly.

'Madam it is made of voile, the finest available. The stitching has been done by a tailoring house in Bombay which is a brand known for its fine work. See, how the fabric falls!'.

She ventured tentatively 'yes, it's nice, but I was wondering how it is priced at two thousand…'

He smiled. 'I will show you something. Look at this, the cut of the gown on the side. The angle of the cut is a little more than what it should have been. It is a fault that will not even be noticed by most, but for a brand it is sacrilegious to sell something like this. Normally they would put it in their factory outlets. So we got it for a throwaway price'.

That's how it was priced so low, it made sense.

But two thousand rupees seemed like an impossible figure for her to get. Assuring the salesman that she would make up her mind and come back, she slunk off. Unlike the Mall Road sales guys who would have never taken her suggestion of coming back some other time meekly, he was genuinely nice saying 'not a problem, am sure we will not get too many customers for the piece, will hold it for you'. Money made people nicer persons, she thought.

All along the way back she could not think of anything else. She knew she would not be able to wear it anywhere. In the social circles that she moved in, gowns were only for little girls. Even teenagers wearing it was frowned upon. Some ladies who had jobs wore *salwar kameezes*, and got away with it. But the rest of them who were housewives were expected in parties and functions only in *saris*. She did not care though. Just to be able to feel the fabric against her skin, even if in the quiet seclusion of her cubby hole of a bathroom, would be enough. In the weeks thereafter, the thought kept weaving in and out through the multiple chores that she did during the day resulting in small disasters, the current one being the salty *poha* and Vijayan going without breakfast.

She got up, could not afford the *sambar* burning especially after the *poha* disaster in the morning. As she passed the kids study table, the small piggy bank sitting on the desk caught her eye. They had started it when Rajan was born. Year after year, as the small clay pig would fill out, Vijayan would get a larger pig and stuff all the accumulated coins into the new one. Never ever, even in the most difficult of times, had he taken a single coin from it. In fact once when her parents-in-law were visiting from the village, what with new clothes to be bought, *puja* to be performed for appeasing the Gods and other sundry expenses, she had suggested they break the piggy bank, he had looked at her as if she was proposing something blasphemous. Now however the pig seemed to be the only thing standing between her and the black gown.

She finished cooking and cleaned the kitchen quickly. The only time available to her was before Vijayan arrived back from office. Rajan had eaten his lunch and gone out to play, he would not be home before a couple of hours; Gita was still at school. She hailed an auto to Mall Road, normally she would have taken the bus, but today she neither had the time nor the patience. Every passing moment terrified her about someone else buying the dress. Though the salesman had promised her, it had been weeks since she had visited him first, she could not expect him to hold off for so long if there were interested customers. Reaching Mall Road, she paid the auto, and almost half-ran through the narrow road towards the alley. Just a block before the shop, she stopped to gather herself and take a breath, it would not do to arrive in the shop in this state. She smoothened her hair and walked up slowly. At the glass pane near the door, she froze. The dress was gone. In its place the mannequin was wearing a skirt and blouse. Her heart plummeted a thousand feet down. In a trance she walked into the shop. The salesman was sitting behind the counter reading a Hindi novel. On seeing her, he got up and said 'Madam, it's so good to see you again'. Saying that, he went behind a wooden cupboard and retrieved a packet. From inside it, he pulled out what was the most beautiful sight to Latha's eyes. The black dress looked even more inviting stretched over the long counter. It was as if a thousand flowers suddenly blossomed in her heart. Now came the difficult part.

'There is a small problem. I actually have just nineteen hundred rupees, a hundred short of the price'. If he declined to give the dress at that price, she would be both, mortified at having made the request and depressed at coming so close to getting it and failing. The accumulated savings from Rajan's regular coin dropping had come to nineteen hundred; initially she had not been sure if it made sense to ask for a discount, but then she decided to take the chance.

He kept quiet and fingered his chin. After a minute or so of unbearable silence, he smiled as if coming to terms with whatever decision he had been trying to make, and said 'ok Madam'. Just like that. No expressions of shock or anger, no bargaining, not even the supercilious look of having given a favour. Latha was in a moment of disbelief. And then she could not wait to grab the packet and leave.

The ride home was a blur. She arrived home to see that neither Vijayan nor Rajan and Gita were back yet. Locking the bedoom door, she sat on the bed and unwrapped the packet. The dress fell out, with its soft, velvety material jarring against the old cotton of the bedspread. For a minute she just sat there fingering the material and feeling it against her cheeks. Then she slowly undressed, completely, so that nothing stood between her and the gown, and put it on. There was only one long mirror in the house, and it was in the bathroom. The bathroom was too small to get the right distance from the mirror for a full length view. Frequently when she dressed for a party and had to check herself in the mirror, she felt frustrated at not being able to stand in the tiny bathroom without creasing a fold or two. Today however she did not mind. As her reflection glided onto the mirror, she saw a lady there. A woman, a well-preserved, shapely woman. The woman had a figure that was neither thin nor fat. She was not beautiful, but there was a certain grace in her features that was unmistakable. The black strapless dress sat on her as though it was fitted to order. There was something about the entire picture that had an aura of – Latha groped for the word, and suddenly it struck her – class. The reflection smiled.

'Ma, where's my piggy bank' Rajan's shout came through the rickety bedroom door. Hell was about to break loose. But Latha's cup was full. She was ready to face the world.

NIRVANA

I

The threshold had the crack for as long as she could remember. And she always liked to poke her foot in. It was as if it was there, and she had to. Something akin to what someone had said about Mount Everest, it was there and hence he had to climb it. She remembered, her teacher had told it while recounting the stories of brave adventurers. It wasn't very different for her. Every time she poked her foot into the crack, she felt a sense of adventure and anticipation. As if there was a whole new universe inside it with galaxies and stars orbiting at the speed of light years, empty space with the ink blue darkness enveloping the celestial bodies, and the earth in it, with cities, towns and villages and one village named Gobindpur, having a girl poking her foot into the crack of a threshold. The whole idea fascinated her.

Beyond the threshold, the first room which led to the rest of the house was the one her grandfather used to entertain his friends, crotchety old men who came in at dawn-break with their toothless mouths grinding the *paan* effortlessly and spewing red betel juice into a brass holder kept on the side. Their arrival heralded calls for tea and the old cook muttering curses under his breath, would get up from his warm bed in the kitchen most unwillingly. The smell of hot, milky tea would waft into the room after some time and she could almost see the old men in the room inhaling the smell as if to warm their bones. The room gave way to a sunken courtyard in the middle of the house, typical of village houses, with rooms surrounding it in a circular fashion, and one path between rooms leading off to the backyard. The rooms were small and choc-a-bloc with the daily necessities that accumulate in a house over years of living – one end of the bed was stacked with quilts, pillows, bedsheets, old and unused blankets to be used on the bed during winters. The table was full of Mother's knick-knacks, Grandmother's sewing things stuffed into a wicker basket, old irons, letters from estranged sons of the family, old Hindi novels. But she never felt the untidiness, smallness or darkness of the rooms. For her the familiarity of the country mattress she could bury her face into and cry, the dusty and broken toys under the cot she would pull out during hot summer afternoons when everyone was sleeping, the torn calendar with Hanuman's picture on it fluttering in the breeze from the fan, signified acquaintance and comfort. Her sisters-in-law perennially complained about the dripping roof, the size of the room, the uneven floor, but she could not understand why they did so, to her all those things meant home. Her mother unlike most other mothers-in-law did not scold her daughters-in-law or chastise them for their comments. On the contrary, she would stretch her legs out on the verandah before the kitchen, issuing orders to the cook, rolling out country cakes called *pithas* and packing sweetmeats for the neighbours. Her childhood had been a protected one, she was the only daughter, her father doted on her, one of her brothers – the one just older to her – went along with her to school. One or the other sister-in-law was always at hand to make hot *parathas* for her when she came from school. She was a good student, unlike most of the other girls in her class who were always giggling over some silly gossip, the teachers always gave her example.

As she grew up, the house acquired another set of overtones. The coconut tree-lined path leading to the mossy pool in the lower backyard, the haystacks in the upper backyard neatly symmetrical, the nooks and corners around the house, all started to hold promises of forbidden pleasure. It was around that time that Ramesh started visiting their house. He was a cousin twice or probably thrice removed, she was not too sure. He had first dropped in with a message and a bundle of home-made *ghee* and *aarisa* sent by his mother. Thereafter he would find excuses to keep coming – on his way to the college in the nearby town, while visiting a friend who stayed nearby, on the pretext of giving some package to her mother sent by his mother. She found him irritating at first, she was a good student and his presence was a drain on her time. Slowly however he started to grow on her and she began to look forward to his visits. The old house accorded many nooks and corners, the mud-baked granary was a favoured spot, so also the thick trees in the backyard with branches camouflaging the empty spaces within them. He was not great at academics but had a very clear world view, and a rebellious one at that. Articulate in the native tongue he would hold on for hours on almost any subject under the sun, starting from what was wrong with the American policy of disarmament to why communism needed to be revived. Good only in curriculum, she would listen to him awed and conscious of a growing sense of enchantment. She was never sure if she fell in love with him, if someone had asked her at that point of time on the uppermost feeling in her mind, it would have been a concoction of being magnetized and of floating in the dark space above stratosphere with the stars only for company. And yet while clearly he seemed taken in by her, he never ever alluded to anything which indicated a lasting relationship. Desperately she would search for words that might hint that he desired permanency in the relationship too but was probably too proud to say so. The words never came. What did come however were proposals from nearby villages for her hand in marriage. They were good proposals, her father was very well off and she would get a handsome dowry being the only daughter in four sons. She could not understand him, in public he would join in on her marriage discussion with as much nonchalance as a regular relative, in private when both were together he would give her a grave smile and just touch her chin. She could have concluded that it was because he thought he was not wealthy enough, but that was not the case, his family was far richer than hers with vast tracts of land reaching till where the eye could not see. Only once she heard him say 'some relationships should just stay that way, we should not try to give it what the society thinks is its logical end, the deliciousness comes from its being vague and transient'. That day she knew she could never think of a life with him. He had robbed her of even the pleasure of fighting for love and losing, she was not even sure if it was love.

Today marriage and the twenty-five years after it seemed like a quick flashback. Her husband had been the average clerical city dweller. There had been the small pleasures and disappointments of life, no event that was uplifting, no tragedy that made her a heroine. Then children came, and school, college followed in quick succession. All these years though she had visited home often, it would be for a marriage or some ceremony with the full family in tow. Today after twenty five years, she had come alone, on the occasion of her father's death anniversary, since her husband was out of city and the children away at hostels. The house was quiet, after her mother had died, two of her brothers had shifted to the city under the guise of setting up new businesses, one brother met an untimely death and his wife had preferred to shift out with her children to her parents' house. Only one brother stayed on with his wife, he was childless, the house would now never reverberate with echoes of children's laughter, the shouts to the cook to make *pithas,* the sound of grain being threshed in the backyard. She sighed. All the familiar nooks and corners were there as they were earlier, only a little dusty and cobweb ridden. Some long forgotten images arose in her mind, a head resting on a broad white-shirted chest, a snatch of conversation spoken in whispers, fair and long fingers intertwined with wheatish large ones. None of their conversations had been about the future, she could not really blame anybody.

She wondered about tomorrow. She wondered what they would do. She had no plan in mind. It was possible that nothing may happen. Or else, a lot could. The only thing was, she would this time be guided by her heart. She would go its way, no questions asked.

II

The *bai* had played truant again. The morning rush to make breakfast and tiffin boxes for the kids and spouse was compounded by the *jhadoo pochha* she had to factor in. In the process she got late for school. The Principal looked at her dagger-eyes behind his horn-rimmed spectacles – 'Mrs. Mohanty you are late again'! As if she didn't know that. Not that this was something new. At least five times in a month she got those looks from him when she went to sign the register. She wanted to tell him at times 'let me see you bring up two kids, manage one spouse, one errant maid, all on a shoestring household budget in a paint-peeling Government quarter and still try to hold down a teacher's job and be on time, and then we can talk'. Maybe today she would tell him. She had nothing to lose, further ahead.

School was generally a pleasure and somewhere she loved the mundane routine, but not so today. A strange restlessness gripped her, urging her to finish her classes as soon as possible and move on. Usually she spent time with the students, explaining things to them on the board, asking additional follow-up questions and testing their ability. Her classes were choc-a-bloc, no one missed it. She was quite an adept teacher. However today was different. She felt irritated at any student who asked a question and thus delayed her. Her annoyance was evident to her pupils, one by one they clammed up and quietly listened, not interrupting her or asking natural queries. Inwardly she chided herself. The bus left only at five in the evening, and her finishing a class early would in no way expedite her departure. However she tried to finish the last class early so that she could go home and pack.

The Principal was sitting quietly and writing something in a fat notebook when she went to sign the register on her way out. She wished he would say something, she was itching to give an acerbic rejoinder. He did not even stir. Silently she willed him to say something, anything. Nothing happened, and finally after a long drawn out signature she was going to step out, when he suddenly said 'so Mrs. Mohanty, you are leaving early today? Is coming late and leaving early the new workplace rule?' Anger bubbled up inside her like a new volcano. She always was the last one to leave, but never ever had he acknowledged it. One day she was leaving early and that was immediate to catch his eye. She turned around and walked back to his desk in measured steps. He looked up at her sound, slightly surprised, he had not expected her to answer him. 'Actually Sir' she said leaning onto his desk 'the new workplace rule is not to answer to intellectually challenged superiors. I have decided to follow this dictum from today onwards'. She smiled at his agape face and walked out, a song in her heart.

She had cleaned the house in the morning itself, there would not be time in the evening after coming back from school, with the bus to catch and all. Also in addition to lunch, she had made dinner, and some extra dishes which they could have with both rice and *roti*. She never knew when she would be back, or whether she would be. Shaking herself free of thoughts that had the potential to bind her down she got down to the business of packing. Thankfully school had been relatively strain free. She taught mathematics, had been a brilliant student in school, especially maths where she always scored cent per cent, so teaching happened without effort. Her teachers in school had very high hopes from her – doctor, engineer, IAS officer – all were aspired-for vocations for her, depending on what that particular teacher was partial to. She used to smile at them, secure in the knowledge that she was very clear on where she wanted to go. A Chair Professor at one of the best Universities abroad, that was her dream. Leafy walkways, Anglo Saxon buildings with high-ceilinged classrooms, all-night cafeterias where debates on semantics stretched long into the night, a university quarter with creeping ivy on the roof – a bitter smile inched up her expression remembering desires long forgotten, hopes long crushed. By becoming a teacher she had somehow tried to mock destiny, to demonstrate what a poor caricature of her dreams she was living. Somewhere along the line she got to love what she was doing and it was primarily because of the kids. What she taught she could do with her eyes closed, it was high school maths, year on year the same old formulae done the same way. A couple of times she tried to innovate on the job, teach a different method to the same old problems. It was invigorating for her. But she left off when she saw it only confused the poor kids.

Everything else happened on the sidelines – marriage, kids – she always felt like a bystander watching herself go through the motions in what most people would consider the most significant aspects of their lives. She played the game by the rules, but it never touched the core of her soul. Even kids, other than the moral obligation of not leaving two small people to fend for themselves, she would not feel any so called tug at her heartstrings if she had to leave them today as long as she knew they would be cared for by the family. She always felt like a star in the galaxy, living a solitary existence, unbound to anything except the sun, which she could never attain.

Her chain of thoughts broke at the shrill sound of the calling bell. This must be the auto-rickshaw driver, she had asked him to come sharp at four. Her packing was done. Casting a quick glance on whether she had packed all cooked food stuff in the fridge, she stuck a post-it on it saying 'going to village' – she had already informed them that she would be going to the village to attend her friend's father's death anniversary function. What she had not mentioned was when she would be back. A wry smile spread across her face. She did not know about the other two, but she was very clear on her next steps.

III

Even after so many years the jet lag hit her. She got down from the plane, picked her bags from the carousel, dumped them in the boot and settled down for a long two hour ride. She might as well sleep, it would be midnight in New Jersey. She smiled at the thought of New Jersey, it had been a great business trip, but more so it had been a personally gratifying experience. She still could feel the warmth of David's smile on her face, the intimate conversations over endless coffee, the multiple art galleries they visited, the intellectual stimulation he brought her. Not all acquaintances ended like this. Sometimes she ran into rude, boorish, or even worse, mundane people, she hated mediocrity. She could withstand eccentricity, quirkiness, but the pedantic irritated her. Hence the life she lived, helped – a high profile role in a multinational company, endless business trips – some of them outside India and even to exotic locales – a single life in the city, far from parents and home, it all suited her. She never could have borne a boring life married to the same person for years together, cooking and cleaning for the kids, a family to come home to every evening. For her, life had to be full of surprises, every single day. She loved the freedom her singleness gave her – she could chose to spend a quiet evening at home with a coffee and some Jagjit Singh *ghazals* or else to go out and have a wild partying night with her friends. There was no compulsion to get up early, unless of course she had a business meeting. She could pack and leave within a moment's notice without a thought of having to take care of someone at home. She wore what she wanted to, unless of course she was going to visit her parents in the village.

Initially her parents had not given up hope on her getting married. After all she had never said she would not, in so many words. She just kept avoiding the issue whenever they asked her, citing work and travel, it helped that she was far away and all conversations were on phone or on the blue inland letters they posted and she never answered. Her few and far in between visits home were too short and too cluttered with visits to relatives for any productive discussion on marriage. Only at night when they sat down to dinner it would give her parents some time to reopen the topic. As she went higher up in her organization, it became easier for her to say that she would be glad to marry if they could find someone suitable, knowing fully well that staying in the village they could not even hope of finding someone who was equal in status. It was a mean trick, but she did not feel guilty about it. It was a small price to pay for keeping them at bay. After some time they left off pushing her. Adjusting to the idea that she would probably never ever get married, they decided to count their blessing – the fat money order that came every month from her. It had eased life quite a bit, more so as the son had stayed back in the village to help the father look after the meagre lands they possessed. The income was minimal.

In the last one year however, she had started feeling strangely discontented with life. It was not just any one thing. While work was fine, there were no new challenges, no surprises that used to occur with amazing alacrity in the early years of her career. She had visited most of the places that she had dreamt of when she was a school girl, the wanderlust was slaked in her. Plus, in the last few months she had started to experience a lack of enthusiasm for travel. This was something so unlike her that first she thought she had hit the midlife crisis or the burnout point or simply menopause. Earlier when she started to travel because business demanded it, she was not too happy with the frequent hotel stays, the packing at a moment's notice, the cramped seating in the plane, but slowly she started getting used to it, and then started enjoying it. Now she had a sense of *déjà vu*, as she started getting irritated with the frequent flier mails. The only difference was earlier it was inconvenient for her to travel; now she was simply not enthused. She just felt drained of energy to make so many changes so frequently. 'Am I growing roots or what' she kept asking herself. She declined a couple of requests to travel and when she declined a third one, a relatively important one from a business point of view, and deputed a junior to travel instead, Avinash called her to his cabin. Avinash was her boss two levels up, but in many ways she was his protégé. He had hired her and even though he was not her immediate reporting manager, she knew he always kept a tab on her, checking on her performance, whether timely promotions happened, asking her about her personal plans whenever they bumped into each other at a social do. With him she could share her inner thoughts and apprehensions without fear of any consequence at the workplace.

'So looks like our Supergirl has hit a wall' he joked waving her into a seat as soon as she entered his cabin.

'I am not too sure Avinash, of what it really is' she replied sinking into one of those plush leather chairs in the corner instead of the hard-backed ones in front of him. 'I just don't feel like travelling, and before you dismiss it off as burnout, stress, boredom with role etc, let me tell you, it's just not work. Am generally in a state of inertia. The travel thing is just one piece'.

'Hmmm' Avinash stuck his interlaced fingers beneath his chin, a sign that he was into a deep dive. He was like that, he would initially assess whether the problem was a relatively simple one which could just get eased off with some counselling, minor changes etc. If it wasn't, he would not offer a superficial solution. She loved him for that.

'When did you last go home' the question was so unexpected that it took her unawares. Avinash knew she was hardly the home-visiting types, and he always advised her to follow her heart. She was surprised why he had sprung the question.

'Quite some time back, actually seven years to be precise' having said it, she was struck by how strange it would be to anyone to have not gone home for that long. But not Avinash, he would understand.

'Do you feel like a visit' he asked looking her in the eye.

And in that moment, she knew she had to go. She had no clue why, or what she would do there. There was hardly anyone else in the village she knew as friends and neighbours, her parents had passed away sometime back, and her brother's

family were not too interested in her visits, few and far in
between as they were, except when her luggage opened and
the gifts came out. That had also been one of the reasons for
no compulsions being there to go except to pay the annual
costs for tax, water and other small repairs. Yet now she
could vividly remember the cowdung washed courtyard
with the huge tree in the corner spreading its branches and
shade all over. Even today she was not quite sure what tree
it was, her botany had always been poor, it had been a sore
point with her father. She remembered the three rooms
facing the verandah, as you stepped up from the courtyard.
The rooms had been small and in a row, when she was in
her teens she would always argue with her father on why
someone should build rooms in a line, and he would answer
'because a straight line is the best geometrical pattern'. He
was so set in his ways, and somewhere she knew she was
more like him than she cared to admit. He had been a strong
virile man, her father, till the end of his days, and somewhere
she had measured all men who had come close to her against
him, and found them coming up short. One of the reasons
why she could not settle down with anyone. Just then she felt
a terrible longing to be back in the shade of that unknown
tree, in that courtyard looking over the three small rooms
in a row. It was an urge so sudden and urgent that it was
almost like a wave of passion washing over her. She looked
up to see Avinash watching her with a half smile lurking at
the corners of his lips.

'Go home, sometimes the answers come from the place
where it all started'.

That day itself she had called the only two other souls she could think of when it came to where it all started. They would also come, it would be a reunion of sorts. What more? That time alone would tell.

IV

It was the old pond where they used to meet when life was simple and uncomplicated. After-school hours used to be spent with the three of them eating the purple-staining *jamun* from the old gnarled tree and chattering on every subject under the sun. Whenever there used to be trouble – boyfriend problem, teacher trouble, punishment over missed assignments – the old *jamun* tree used to be their solace. Somehow while troubles did not disappear under it, answers always became clearer. Whether parents were to be told the truth about the fudged marks or not, whether the matinee was worth missing the afternoon class for, which could be the 'possible' questions that the crochety History teacher would set for the exam – questions which otherwise seemed unsurmountable to the teenage mind, lent themselves to answers more easily. It was but natural that they converge at the same spot. They had not asked each other to meet there; but somehow they all knew, they would meet there at four in the evening. When school used to end. And the dust raised by the returning cattle on the village *kutcha* roads used to spread a thin veneer on the setting sun as it sunk into the pond beyond the tree. The pond used to be out of limits for them, it was a very deep one. Unlike the other village ponds, it was never used for washing or bathing. In fact long years ago when a woman had drowned in it while trying to get water, no one ever went near it. Undisturbed, it stood still, as if since time immemorial no one had touched it.

They sat quietly on the broken fence beneath the tree, not speaking a word. There was no need to. They all knew each others' lives threadbare. The setting sun was starting its journey into the depths of the pond. They got up and walked towards it, separate, yet together like one. As they entered the pond, strangely the last thought each one had was whether they would meet the sun at the bed of the pond.

A Life less Ordinary

Every day it was the same. She awoke to the irritating sound of the bell being pressed into the service of God, the sickeningly sweet smell of incense sticks bought from the local *kirana* store and the dull chant of hymn. How someone could go on and on, everyday, without a break, was a wonder to her. It was not as if he seemed fired by devotion. It was the kind of dull and dogged determination to have an hour long *Puja* no matter what, which was annoying. Don't you feel trapped in this ritual you have set for yourself, she wanted to ask him. But she could not, it would skew the balance of their marital life. A false balance maintained on unspoken rules but nevertheless understood on both sides.

Prakash could almost hear the thoughts running through his wife's head. She never told him anything, but he knew the hour long ritual messed up her morning nap after she had seen the kids off to school. She liked to catch up on lost sleep before getting up to make his breakfast before he left for office. He could not blame her, she too had her hands full. Unlike how they showed in movies, the husband was not oblivious to the dull rigour of the housewife. But he had his own circle of monotony and exhaustion to deal with. He wondered why they did not show that in movies, two equally trapped people trying to make the best of circumstances rather than false perceptions about one acting

41

the villain. He had never told her, that the *Puja* was his escape from life. And he suspected she probably understood, somewhere in the deep recesses of her mind. An escape from the everyday routine of home, office and back home, the monotony of the same old work at office with no hint of any new or innovative assignment. In the first few years when the kids were growing up and like all parents they saw glimmerings of genius in every single question the kids asked, the poems they recited, he saw that as his salvation. The kids would grow up and make him proud of them, and then all the boredom that he had suffered through life would be more than made up by the subsequent glory. When it became apparent that the glory would never come because they had mistaken precociousness for genius, his last hope crumbled away. Life was 'there', not happening, but merely existing. At office the days rolled into months with nothing changing, neither the work, nor the colleagues nor even the daily routine they followed. While office started at ten, generally he was the only one to arrive by that time. Not even the boss came in before ten fifteen. Everyone mostly filed in by ten thirty, usually rushing in breathless so as not to be reprimanded by the *Bada babu* for being late, with polythene bags, tiffin carriers, and sundry stuff. The ladies would generally carry some *saris* with *sari falls* to be stitched on, or some other article of clothing, with which they would sneak out to the dressmaker's during lunch time. He envied their preoccupation with their lives – children, husbands, the latest blouse design, vegetable prices – they were so passionate about all the elements that ruled their lives that he was sure they never had a dull moment. Compared to them the men were more staid, they came in with lesser noise, settled their bags and boxes and generally went for a smoke. Not being a smoker, he again lost out on some good natured gossip and ribbing. Frequently he toyed with the idea of joining the club just to be one of them, and in fact he had experimented once. But more than the coughing bout which followed, it was the taste that put him off. They had laughed and slapped him on the back saying 'don't bother, you are different from the lot of riff-raff that's us'. It had hurt. He knew they had meant well, putting him on a higher pedestal than themselves, but the last thing he wanted was to be different. He wanted to get into the same vortex they were in, vocal, opinionated and passionate about so many things, it seemed to make their lives worthwhile. Even the tiffin boxes were so much of a conversation piece, there was always something different everyday in their lunch boxes – sometimes it was the *poori* and the amount of oil it had and how the missus was so negligent about health, other times it could be the *mixed sabji* which was so bland and bereft of *masalas* that was the centrepiece of discussion. He could not contribute, he got the same *rotis, dal, bhindi fry* and *achar*. He could not blame the wife, it was he who had dictated the menu, to be given everyday. But then nothing stopped her from disobeying him, changing it a bit, packing something different without telling him. What choice would he have but to eat it. And it would have brought some fun into their staid lives, but that was not to be, he lacked even that much playfulness in life. It was as if his corner of the office was the most unhappening one, even the wall colours looked more faded than others. His desk was clean and colourless compared to others' which were littered with wrapping papers, glue, colourful stickies, dried and withered flowers.

On certain days he strongly felt that death would be better than a life where the prevalent state was boredom. But he was terrified of the thought that the event of his death would be the ultimate boring incident, tucked away in fine print in some corner of the newspapers, neither exciting nor distressing anyone. The least he wanted was to go out in a blaze of glory as some sort of fitting finale for a life less lived.

It was an unusually warm February afternoon when the boss called him into his cabin. Generally he preferred to walk down to the staff cubicles rather than call them to his cabin – 'it gives some leg-stretch' was his favourite quote. If he called one to his cabin, it was when he wanted his team member to meet some customer or any senior official from corporate. He wondered what it was this time. A faint smell of some kind of wild rose greeted him as he opened the door slowly. A figure in a pale pink and white *sari* was sitting with her back to him in front of the boss. 'Come my boy' the boss waved him into the seat next to the unknown lady. 'Madam here needs some information about our fixed deposit instruments'. Theirs was a small State-owned bank that even in the face of stiff competition from the new age corporate banks still had a loyal clientele. They did give some handsome interest rates especially on fixed deposits, thanks to the long-time relationship the proprietor had with some of his friends in the business community where they invested those funds and got a decent return. They had some old customers who inspite of the spiffy banks in circulation preferred to park their savings in the old but trustworthy bank. But this lady seemed new, he didn't remember seeing her earlier. He turned to take a look at her and as he did, she did the same too. She had the fair, delicate boned structure which he used to hate earlier, and was one of the reasons why he had preferred his wife's robust, dusky and wholesome contours. That was a long time back. He looked again as his boss's voice droned in the background. She did not have features that would fulfil the requirements of classic beauty. However there was some strange elf-like quality in her face which drew him in like a magnet. Framed by softly curling hair that was *hennaed* red, it was a fair and oval face, the nose had a small nose-pin, probably studded with a diamond. Or a white stone. Anyway he would not be able to tell. The *sari* clothed a slim figure that seemed almost girlish in comparison to his wife who had bloated up with each pregnancy. Thin gold bangles adorned slim wrists. A pair of white pearl-studs clung to ears that looked as if they were carved out of alabaster. The lips were not the full voluptuous ones he used to fancy in his youth, but thin ones, and somehow he found it more appealing, with its rose tinted hue. He could not see her feet but he was sure they were slender, smooth – his wife's were always cracked and callused – with toenails painted a light colour encased in a simple but elegant footwear. His wife insisted on wearing sandals in bright red, yellow and equally horrifying colours – which lady wore sandals nowadays – and with toenails in a permanent state of chipped nailpolish, it was a sight he avoided if he could.

He sat in the chair next to her, trying to avoid looking at her. But then his boss asked him to explain the pros and cons of the various fixed deposit schemes they had, and it was but inevitable to look at her. He was already in a cloud of the mildly enticing perfume she wore, but when he turned towards her, it hit him like an avalanche, which was the wrong term to use, because nothing could be gentler or subtler than the smell that hung about her. But its impact on him was like being swept away. Swept away into a world of gently closing curtains, silken white sheets, luxuriously upholstered seats and soft conversations. Almost mechanically – and he thanked his stars that he was so well conversant with the technicalities that he could reel it off while his mind was elsewhere – he told her about the various schemes, the interest percentages, maturity periods and other details. She listened with a detached air, not interrupting nor asking questions, as if understanding but not getting interested in the details, as if her own mind was also elsewhere. The faint smile which was there on her lips was still playing as he spoke about the details. His boss's voice boomed, breaking his train of thoughts; he was thankful for that, else he was not sure what he would have done once his information was exhausted and yet his heart would not make him turn away from her. 'Madam, you think it over' his boss was saying 'once you decide I will get the papers sent to you and you can sign and return them.' 'Sure' he heard a sophisticated yet sweet voice say. The rest of the meeting happened in a haze, he was mildly aware that she thanked him, shook hands with the boss, and left closing the door softly. 'My boy, you look as if you have been hit by a dump truck' his boss burst out laughing. 'Hardly Sir' he said trying to keep his voice even. 'I know, I was just kidding' he replied getting busy with papers on his desk. And the boss meant it, he knew that, in office his reputation was one of being hard-working, honest and boring. No one but no one in the office would even remotely ascribe to him any of the emotions that he was currently undergoing.

He came out to see the men gossiping away about the recently departed customer of the bank. They did not even observe as he came back and sat in his seat. Suddenly Rajesh broke out of the group and turned to him 'What a pity the boss called you, such a waste. Why could he not call me!'. Then he turned back rejoining the discussion and they kept on breaking out into peals of laughter intermittently, pulling each other's leg in good natured ribbing. He felt as if his insides were burning. His whole being revolted at not being considered smart or suave enough for even a casual flirtation. But it was a reputation he had built over time, it wasn't easy to deny it overnight.

That evening as he sat in the bus headed for home, his mind entered a realm of till then unknown possibilities. He marveled at how even in thoughts he never ever strayed beyond the contours of life available to him. 'So foolish' was the thought running over and over in his mind. And to think, he would have been shocked at himself for having such thoughts even a day back. The rest of the evening passed in a haze. Even his wife observed his preoccupation, it was much beyond his usual taciturn ways. 'The *mandi* did not have any good vegetables, had to make do with whatever was there at home' she said. He grunted, as if he had ever made an issue with whatever was served. Generally the kids crowded up to him after dinner for a story, today however he had no patience for anything other than his thoughts. Telling them he was tired and would tell them two stories the next day, he went off to the bedroom. The wife looked askance at him, he could make out even as he walked off with his back to her, after years of staying together he did not need to look at her to know what she was thinking.

The next day morning his usual extended *puja* took much lesser time. He was in a hurry to get to the wardrobe. But as he shuffled through his clothes, he was struck, for the first time, with the scarcity of outfits with him, he could not find one single piece that took his fancy. He tried one shirt, then another, each looked equally washed out to him. His wife came in as he was flinging one shirt after the other on the bed. 'What's wrong' she sounded genuinely surprised 'is there a button missing or something'. In the nineteen years of marriage, except the first few years when the novelty of a new partner had still not worn off, he had never tried a second shirt on while leaving for work. Let alone work, she could not remember an occasion when he had tried on multiple outfits even when going for a party. He could not blame her for feeling surprised.

'No, no, they are fine.' He felt guilty without knowing exactly why.

On the way to office, for the first time, he noticed what the others were wearing, especially the men. All seemed to be better dressed than him. Somehow even the conductor's cheap jeans and canary yellow shirt seemed better than his own brown shirt and grey trousers. He felt despondent, how could he undo instantaneously what years of sloppy dressing and thinking had done to him.

At office it was a busy day and he was thankful for that. He did not get much time to mull over his meeting the day before. Only once when the boss called him to hand over a file, his hopes surged for a moment anticipating it was something to do with the transactions related to the earlier day. But without looking up from the papers he was poring over, the boss just handed him a file saying 'here, take this', it was an old debt issue that he had been handling. As he walked out he thought he sensed a faint remnant of the perfume she had worn the day before.

He left office early that day, slinking off quietly by the back door which most employees used when they came in late or left early. Not that anyone observed, sometimes he felt that were it not for the work he did, most of his colleagues would not even realize that he was there, two hands and a head, working alongside them. Instead of the bus home, he took number thirty-nine which went to the nearby marketplace. After about twenty minutes when he alighted from the bus, he was surprised at the teeming place, choc-a-bloc with hawkers selling sundry things starting from *jasmine* garlands to watermelon slices, shops for toys, groceries, clothes, *thela-wallahs* with bananas, guavas and *chikus* and in the middle of it all, people of all shapes and sizes. For the last few years the only market he went to was the local supermarket for monthly groceries, everything else down to his shirt and pant was bought by his wife. And since he was never particular about what he wore, it had never been a problem. Today faced suddenly with a plethora of choices he felt undone. Gingerly he crossed the thoroughfare and walked into the first lane which seemed relatively quieter with mostly garment shops lined on both sides of the road. At first he just walked down the road, stealing glances at the shops, unable to decide which one to venture into. Some appeared high-class and probably out of his range; in contrast some others seemed cheap and tawdry. Finally he checked out one which seemed to be a quiet one, manned by an elderly benevolent-looking gentleman. 'I am looking for some ready-made shirts and pants' he blurted out, not knowing what else to say. He felt panic-stricken all of a sudden. How would he ask for a certain colour, cut or fabric. He did not have the faintest clue of what suited him, his body type and all those factors which were supposed to be the deciding factors for making a purchase. Somehow the gentleman seemed to understand. He guided him to the cool recesses of the shop and in one corner where stacks of shirts seemed to burst out of the shelves, made him wait while he went over to the other side of the counter, and started to show him shirts in various shades. 'Your size will be 38, you are slim, just check the shades you like and then we can pull out a selection' he said. For once, since the time he had landed in the market place he was not lost. Blue, that had been his favourite colour in college, he wore so many shades of the same colour that his mother used to lose her temper about it. The thought brought a smile to his face. He caressed the fabric, it was soft to the touch, and though certainly not in league of the expensive material some of his colleagues wore to work, was still quite good. Next came the pants, that was easy, he settled for a deep blue that would go with the shirt. 'Excellent choice' the shopkeeper remarked, and although he knew he would be saying that to all his customers in all probability, it still felt good.

Paying the bill, he stuffed the polythene packet in his office briefcase, his wife would know about the purchase sooner or later, but better to delay the point of discovery. His mood swung several notches up as he caught the bus back home. He found himself humming an old tune he had forgotten as the evening breeze from the bus window tousled his hair. As he walked from the bus stop to his house, he tried to rearrange his expression so that it would not give away his emotions. He tried to frown, but somehow it would not stay for more than a few seconds. 'I can always say that I had a great day at office' he thought while he knew how unconvincing it sounded even to him. He had not felt like that in years.

The evening was spent trying to keep an inscrutable expression. Years of a life together had taught his wife to pick out even the slightest deviation in mood. 'What happened in office today' she asked casually as they sat at the dining table. 'The same old, nothing unusual' he replied amazed at her reading his mind instantaneously. 'You seem happier' she murmured and went off into the kitchen to get a dish. He was spared the need of answering, thankfully. He almost felt like a teenager in love for the first time. It was difficult to keep the euphoria from spilling onto his face. After dinner, sensing his ebullient mood, the kids wanted him to do a story-telling for them. All he wanted was to hit the sack and dream about shades of pinks, colognes and wispy clouds. But that would make his wife suspicious, so he played with the kids for some time, told them stories, more so to avoid making conversation with her. He did not want to get into a room with her, it would become crowded. He feigned sleep when she came in. Generally she would make some small talk – the price of onions and tomatoes, the kids at school, the bike not starting/not braking etc – but today she had also sensed something was different. It was awkward lying on his back with his eyes closed when he could feel her eyes on him, so he turned on his side towards the wall. 'Are you okay' she asked just then. 'Yeah' he had never been good at faking, and that also one reason behind the irritation she felt towards him, he knew that. He felt her settle down beside him, but could sense she was wide awake, thinking, worrying. He couldn't care less, finally sleep overtook him and he gladly gave himself up hoping for some respite at least in dreams.

The next morning he overslept. By the time he woke up the kids had left. He threw off the covers and went straight to the bathroom. He came back in the towel and started rummaging for his briefcase. 'Should I get your clothes out' she asked following behind him. 'No, no, its ok'. He felt her eyes boring through him as he fished out the polythene packet from his briefcase. Hurriedly he changed, he was already running late, and he didn't want to miss his breakfast, she would become still more suspicious. 'Where did you get this from' she was serving *parathas* on the table as she asked in a clipped manner. 'The market near the office', he mumbled not wanting to give an explanation which he knew she was waiting for, no point in telling more lies than were needed. 'You could have told me, there would have been a good discount during *Pujas*, its hardly a month away. The fabric would also have been better' she said. He was getting irritated at her effort to prolong the conversation. 'Needed to buy it yesterday, no good clothes' muttering it under his breath, he quickly stuffed the rest of the *paratha* into his mouth and before she could say anything else or thrust one more *paratha* at him, rushed off to wear his shoes. 'Expenses are going to go up, the kids will get into a new session, books and uniforms have to be bought.' He felt thwarted, frustrated. He could not even buy a pair of new clothes for himself without her making him feel guilty about it. She did not want to let go even an iota, not that the daily drudgery gave her any pleasure, but she would not relinquish control. He felt claustrophobic, it was almost a physical feeling of being choked up. If he hadn't left immediately, he felt he would have burst a blood vessel there itself.

The bus was already crowded by the time he got onto it. Thankfully he got a seat, not his favourite window one but a middle one, squashed between another office goer and a middle-aged lady. He tried to close his eyes and go far away from the din and bustle of his surroundings. Escape, that was the only thought swirling in his mind. Escape from the drudgery at office, the constricted atmosphere at home, escape from his daily hot and humid bus rides, the predictable tiffin-box packed by his wife, even from the story-telling sessions with his kids. He felt trapped, horribly trapped. No one told him it would be like this. How would it be to go out of the boundaries of his pedantic life, to have another life, a life which did not have boundaries, where you got to decide the boundaries, where you were not answerable, accountable or responsible. He sometimes saw movies on the television where he saw the protagonist live a life in some far outreaches, eke out a living by the day, go out everyday not knowing what the day would bring him, having new experiences every day. Some years back he would have been appalled had someone even suggested that he live this life. Today it seemed like a dream that could deliver him from all that seemed unworthwhile in life. But there was hope, he smiled to himself as an apparition in pinks enveloped in floral fragrances rose in his mind. He closed his eyes and settled back to give himself up to an hour of pleasurable thinking.

At office he waited impatiently, his mind only half on the work on his desk. It was a Thursday, the day when the bank advertised fixed deposit accounts and gave a point five per cent interest more to anyone who opened an account on the day. The lady had promised to come back today to start her account. Or she would call someone to go to her house with the papers. For important customers, generally who ever handed the portfolio made the home visit. He handed the fixed deposit portfolio. Thrice when the boss rang his bell, he got up in anticipation thinking it was for him, only to have some one else called for. Lunchtime came and went. For once he left his tiffin untouched, he would think up of something to say at home, there was no way he was going to eat *curd rice* while waiting for the doors of freedom to open up for him. The afternoon sun started to slowly go down, its slanting rays mocking him through the cracked glass panes of the office window. He felt something mounting inside him, a sort of build-up of something he could not define, in sometime it would rise to his throat and choke him up. It was now or never, he took her file from his table and almost ran to the boss's cabin. Some colleagues in the side cubicles looked up, it was most unlike him to rush anywhere. He entered the cabin, and then remembered he had forgotten to knock. 'Ah Prakash, come in, I was about to call you'. A hope long forgotten surged in him. 'You remember Mrs. X who came in on Tuesday and wanted to open a fixed deposit with us?'. He almost laughed out loud, remember her, I remember even where the individual strands of her *hennaed* hair lay on her silken head, he wanted to scream at the boss. 'Yes Sir' was all he could manage, thrill making him clutch the file tighter. She was not here, which meant he would be asked to carry the papers to her home. 'Well she called today to say her husband has been transferred to Almora. She still wants to open the account with us, but now she will open it in our Almora branch'.

His mind was blank as he walked back to his seat. A wave of grey washed over him. Almora. There was a map of all the bank branches stuck on the softboard in everyone's cubicle. He looked at it. There was one tiny red dot on Almora. He remembered, they always had an issue in getting anyone posted to Almora. Neither could they get educated localites to join. It was a very small office with a couple of staff. If he took a transfer there, he would be posted as Branch Manager. They even gave a raise to anyone willing to go there as an incentive. Almora. In the hills. With none of the heat and dust of the plains he underwent every day. Gentle. Wispy. Fragrant. Elusive. And he could not take his wife and kids along, she would not agree to interrupting their studies. And she need not even know that he had asked for it, a transfer was generally interpreted as something that was a directive. In fact, given the raise, she may take it as a positive development. He smiled, all was not lost. Almora, sounded like a lost kingdom which he was about to reclaim.

THE BALCONY

It was a verdant balcony. As verdant as a balcony can get. His daughter-in-law Bhagya had planted small pots with crotons, tea roses, the ubiquitous money plant, the sweet smelling night jasmine which gave a heady odour in the still evenings laden with an oppressive warmth, and some *pudina,* and *hari mirchi* for her kitchen needs. One wall was lined with false green bamboo to give the effect of enveloping greenery. A real vine twisted around it, its tendrils extending till the window that separated the balcony from the living space. That was what he didn't like, its proximity to the living space. The living space was a den of noise and clamour, with his son Raghav, daughter-in-law Bhagya and even their ten-year old son Rahul making it an entertainment area on most evenings. It disturbed his peace and he felt like a five-year old deprived of his candy. It wasn't as if it was a big balcony too, would hardly be a ten by twelve feet area. But it felt like a haven. And it was not only because of the plants alone, though that was a big part of it. It was also the rickety chair he had retrieved from the old house when they had moved, his son was completely against bringing it.

'Baba, why do you need this old thing, it's falling to pieces. We will buy a new one for you, maybe one of these new age recliners, they look so good' Raghav had argued.

He did not tell him that he feared the recliner would reject him. And even if it didn't, how funny would they look together. So he insisted and for once got his way. He would have told his son the rickety thing occupied less space on the balcony, any day lesser than the modern day recliner, which was just as well for the tiny balcony. It sat in a corner with no cushions – his daughter-in-law said it was a hassle, what with her having to keep a tab on rains which would wet the cushions – quietly awaiting his arrival everyday.

He had a daily routine. He had to get up early so that Bhagya could serve him breakfast before she left. She was a good girl, managing both office and house, and so he didn't feel like telling her that it was too early for him to have breakfast, and that he just didn't feel like eating so early. Or that while he appreciated her attempts at *dosa* and *idlis*, it only served to remind him of the white, fluffy *idlis* or the crisp, brown *dosas* of his wife. The house became empty by nine in the morning, all having left for office and school. That's when he settled down in the balcony with the morning newspapers. It was his favourite time of the day. Especially if it was a cloudy day with a light breeze. His son had put a fan in the balcony so that when they socialized with friends and it was a large crowd, they could use the balcony. But most of the time he didn't need it. Even though it was a warm place, he had sensed a gradual chill settling on his bones as the days went by. He almost never used the air-conditioner they had set up in his room, but it was the fan he hated most, with its whirring sound and its speed. It almost reminded him of attributes that he would now never possess. The sun slanted in, first dappling the potted plants that were planted in pots on iron stands projecting out of the balcony and some inside it, then going on to stretch it's reach to touch the far end where he sat. It was always an unsaid battle, how quickly would the sun reach his chair and compel him to seek refuge inside the house. On rainy or cloudy days, when the sun didn't rise at all, he had the last laugh. He would sit in the balcony practically the entire day, browsing through all the papers in detail, till the maid came and jousted him out of his seat. Sometimes he slept in the chair if the weather permitted, his spectacles askance, the papers strewn in disarray on the floor. Not that the chair was anyway comfortable for sleeping. But he hated the cold, clinical bedroom, with its pastel coloured curtains, striped bedsheet and carpeted floor. The old house they had stayed in when his wife was still alive and he had not retired, had floral bedsheets – his wife had been partial to floral prints, and though he had not particularly liked them at first, he grew used to it – the curtains were made out of her old Mysore saris, he could spot some familiar stains in them, one when she had accidentally dropped *sambhar* in her first official party at his colleague's place, another when she first fried fish for him, a real first since she was a *pucca* vegetarian, and had singed the *pallu* in one place. The floor had been red oxide, cool to the feet, polished to a shine by her. She did not believe in keeping servants; when he had insisted that all his colleagues' wives, even though housewives, employed domestic help, her reply had been a tart 'lazy gossip-mongers all'. She ran a tight household and that's how they had been able to give Raghav a good education. That did not mean she did not have her small set of luxuries. She loved her Mysore silks, that's how they had such a truckload of old ones to make curtains! The daily jasmine string in her hair was a must, its pungent aroma filling the spaces wherever she went. The weekly dose of *idli, dosa, uthapam* was also *de rigeur*.

They had been shocked when he accepted her death with equanimity. Raghav interpreted his silent acceptance as a possible trauma that had hit him. It took him some time to convince everyone around him, that he was fine; he could see that they found it a trifle odd. He didn't blame them, after all their closeness to each other was known. He himself was not surprised though. Malathi was a part and parcel of him, irrespective of whether she was present bodily or not. Even today he could smell the faint odour of her jasmine string. He spoke to her as he always did when she was alive, only he took care not to vocalize, they would only see it as a sign of advancing senility. The best time for extended conversation was when he settled down in his chair in the morning after everyone had left. Even then he took care to have the conversation only in mind – once when he inadvertently moved his lips while speaking, the maid had given him an odd look. After that he never ever did a lip sync for his thoughts.

Malathi had understood his penchant for the chair. She chided him gently, but he knew it was her affection and concern. It had been the same when he would indulge in an extra *dosa*, she would pull him up blaming his lack of discipline for his diabetes. And then she would make an extra one, without oil and ply him. 'It's not the same as the one with oil, you know' he would say just to irritate her. The thought brought a smile to his lips. Now of course he ate *dosas* in olive oil, it did not matter if he ate an extra one, but somehow he never wanted an extra.

Apart from the maids who came in to do the sundry household chores, there was no other interruption during the day. There was one who came to do the cooking for lunch, she did not disturb him except calling out after she finished 'have your lunch, it's on the table'. Once the *jhaddo pochha* maid finished, there was a lull for a long time. Unlike others in his age group, he never regretted the long stretches of silence that stretched before him till afternoon. On the contrary, he dreaded the loudness of arrivals starting late afternoon. His grandson arrived at about two in the afternoon with a loud banging of doors that sometimes woke him from a light post-lunch sleep. He liked having him around, but he hated having his reverie broken. And in fact till Bhagya came back from work at about six in the evening, Rahul was his responsibility. He had to ensure he changed his dress, had his food, did his homework, then went out to play etc. 'It is also good engagement for you Baba' Raghav had said when the routine was established, no doubt expecting that he would welcome the diversion. He dared not tell him that the rickety chair in the balcony and his conversations with Malathi were his world, he could never ever feel bored with that. Sometimes he forgot to ensure Rahul changed his dress, and he could sense the mild chide in Bhagya's voice 'Baba, Rahul has not even changed his school dress…'. He felt guilty on such occasions. After all they were good, his son and daughter-in-law, taking care of all his needs and comforts, not in the sense of just discharging a responsibility, but actually making him a part of whatever they did. It was very little that they asked in return. Why could he not even do that. On one occasion Rahul had fallen asleep without having his lunch, and he could see the question in Raghav's eyes. They had taken him for an Alzheimer's test too. While they told him that the results were normal, he did not completely believe them. He saw his daughter-in-law issuing instructions to Rahul to have his lunch on his own without waiting for Grandpa to serve it to him. He could also hear frequent phone calls after Rahul came back from school, and from the conversation on this side he could sense that it was Bhagya asking him whether he had changed, had his food etc. It was probably true, he had also been feeling a sense of memory slipping away from him lately. He would suddenly go blank when his son came and asked him something innocuous. There were spots of time when he was not able to fathom where he was and what he was doing. When he was small, similar signs with elderly people would be dismissed as absentmindedness, common to old age. Now he wondered if these weren't the beginning signs of Alzheimer's. He remembered old men and women sitting in stupor in the mud verandahs in front of the house in his village. The children had to care for them, almost to the last daily ablution. No one complained, it was understood as a part of one's responsibility. Once he remembered one old man had gone missing from the village. For weeks together they could not trace him. His son registered a case in the local police station. Finally after almost a month of disappearance, the police brought him back, unkempt, dirty and stinking from afar. But on reaching his house the man got such a look of terror in his eyes that for a moment they all felt as if the police had brought the wrong person. He refused to go into the house, refused to recognize his son and simply sat in the front verandah staring blankly ahead. Not knowing what to do, they then took to feeding him where he sat, and even cleaned him up there itself. First he resisted, spitting out the food, thrashing about when they tried to bathe him. But slowly as hunger took over, he let them do as they please, noisily chewing the food, with saliva dripping from the corners of the mouth. It lasted for about three weeks at the most, he again ran away. After that they never found him. Somehow he sensed that the family was secretly relieved. The burden of caring for him for those three weeks, when he even soiled himself unknowingly and they had to draw a makeshift curtain in the verandah to shield themselves while cleaning him up, had taken its toll. There was no police complaint lodged, and the village *Sarpanch* who had been following up on his return, also left off after some time.

He was terrified that he would end up doing something similar, running away from home, never to be found again. Of course he had no doubts that Raghav would turn the world upside down to find him, but then you never know, the world was such a large place, what if they did not find him. What if he ended up somewhere, soiling himself, eating out of dustbins, walking around in a stupor, not knowing his name, undignified and uncared for. He shivered at the mere prospect. He started locking the door against himself, checking and rechecking once the maids came and left. He became irritable when Rahul would go to play leaving the front door open. Any slight forgetfulness on his part terrorized him. Once Raghav had given him the car keys to be kept in the drawer – they were going to a party in a friend's car – and when he asked him for it once they were back, for the life of him he could not remember where he had kept it. Finally Raghav only fished it out from over the refrigerator, but he just could not get over it, asking himself again and again 'how could I forget, how could I forget'. 'Baba, why are you worrying so much, this is a small thing' Raghav tried to assuage him. But he was petrified, thinking that it was just the beginning of a larger phenomenon.

The only time when he felt he was in full possession of his faculties was when he was in the rickety chair on the balcony. Every single thing that had happened in his life passed as a mental image with not a single miss. He felt if he could search for all answers from the same place, not ever would they find him missing anything. Mostly he could do that, no one generally came to disturb him from the place. Even after everyone was home, they occupied other places in the house – Rahul in his room playing with toys, Bhagya in the kitchen, Raghav generally in the living room, which though adjacent to the balcony, did not pose a problem since he worked quietly most of the time – and left him to his peace and quiet. The only exception was when they had parties. People thronged the dining space, the kitchen, the living space spilling out onto the balcony. Could not blame them, the bedrooms were off limit, and the only other balcony in the house was used for drying the washing and stored sundry other household materials. And one balcony was needed in any case for the smokers. They puffed away cigarette after cigarette until the smoke completely obliterated the pungent jasmine aroma that always hung in the air, for him at least. The parties happened late by which time Rahul was generally in bed. He was the only odd one out. On the first few occasions he had actually tried to mingle – Raghav had told him categorically that he should socialize, all his friends knew that his father stayed with him, and it was nothing to be hidden. But soon he realized he would only spoil their fun. The moment they saw him, they would immediately snuff out their cigarettes, turn down the music, greet him, talk to him and try and make him comfortable. He smiled internally, they were good people, but they were here to, what they called, 'let their hair down', he didn't want to spoil their evening. Whenever there was a party, he would feign he wanted to have an early dinner, and retire to his room. He had difficulty falling asleep, the clamour seeped in like a hydra, settling in, at every nook and corner of the room. But he didn't mind that so much. What simply wouldn't go away was the thought of smoke enveloping the balcony, the plants and someone sitting on his old rickety chair. He would try and shut his eyes tight, as if that somehow would shut his mind also to undesirable thoughts.

He would never forget the day Raghav came home with the news that he had been transferred to another city. They needed to wrap up things quickly, his replacement would come to stay in the house within a month. His first thought was of the balcony. How could he leave it behind. And the rickety chair, he was sure Raghav would not allow him to carry it, they had left things in far better condition back in the old house when they had shifted last time. Gingerly he asked Raghav 'will the new house have a balcony?'. 'How do I know Baba, have I seen it yet? You also, sometimes…' Raghav trailed off. Generally Raghav was never short-tempered with him, on the contrary he was more patient with him than he was with Rahul at times. But nowadays what with work at office, extra work due to the shifting, he came home looking hassled all the time. Poor fellow, must not be easy on him to handle a doddering father on top of that. His mother knew how to handle him. Before Raghav's marriage and when Malathi was alive, he would come home and sit down near his mother's feet as she chopped vegetables, strung a *jasmine* garland or watched television. She would knead his hair slowly and then give him some of her *chamomile* tea, she made it herself – not the off-the-shelf variety which was served in other households – from leaves she procured from God knows where, dried and stored in airtight ceramic containers. It always worked. It was different now.

He was not sure if it was the looming thought of the receding balcony that led to more forgetfulness on his part. Suddenly his ability to remember things plummeted. He started forgetting whether he had brushed his teeth in the morning. Where he had kept the newspapers. Why he was wearing a towel and standing in front of the bathroom. First it was these small things. Then one day he could not recognize Raghav for a full ten minutes, before finally some glimmerings of memories long buried, rushed in to save the day. That night he cried into his bed until the wee hours of the morning. By the time the early light of the sun glinted off the window panes, he had made his decision. Living with what slowly seemed to be becoming a full blown case of Alzheimer's was not what he wanted. But what was the alternative. He was not the suicidal types. On the other hand a couple of times after he emerged from momentary lapses of memory, the very brief period where all memories were blanketed out seemed like a snow-covered, quiet and heavy landscape, a haven of sorts. And as the days passed, he seemed to want more and more to get into that refuge, where there were no monsters chasing him, a quiet and kind place where he was not answerable to anyone including himself. He remembered reading somewhere that the after effects of cocaine or any of the barbiturates similarly took the drug user to a place of sunshine and light, flight and fantasy. He felt the same way, as if he had gone to a place of lightness and brightness and come back. The real world was fraught with question marks, puzzled expressions on others' faces and irritation at himself. In the beginning he tried to hide the obvious memory lapses as a matter-of-fact issue. Considering his age these also got dismissed off as old age problems. However after some time they became too frequent to go unnoticed. 'Baba, the front door is open and so are all the bedroom doors, did you not close it after the maid left?' Raghav had come home that day during the afternoon as he had to babysit Rahul, Bhagya was going to be late. Two days after that they found him sitting silently staring into vacant space as the rice grew cold on his plate. The instances had grown. He did not like the worried look on Raghav's face when he looked at him. He knew what must be going on in his mind – the turn of events as his father's condition would steadily worsen, which was but inevitable. He felt torn between disappearing into oblivion into the whiteness of nothingness in his rickety chair in the balcony, and trying to keep himself from slipping for the sake of Raghav. And now that Raghav had told him that they were shifting, he felt terrified at the thought of the balcony slipping away from him.

The house had become a hubbub of activity. Clothes in various stages of packing lay strewn around everywhere. Cutlery, pots, pans, Rahul's toys, footballs, plastic *dabbas*, the medicine box – all were in various stages of disarray as Bhagya ran around the house trying to keep things running in the midst of the packing. Two people from the movers and packers were busy sorting things into separate piles, and then tying them up in neat brown packets, scotch-taped and labelled. No one paid much attention to him, even Raghav was busy rifling through his files, disposing off unwanted papers, filing office and home papers separately and going through his clothes and stuff to take only what was needed. The situation was reminiscent of his young days when his father had become old and decrepit – he remembered taking care of him, but not really thinking his opinion was needed on any matter. Come to think of it, he had not had any more importance than a piece of furniture in the house, one which needed caring, but need not be consulted for anything. It was ironic how life had come full circle.

The next few days passed in a blur. The terror of going to a balcony-less house where he would have no place to sit out his whiteness had become all encompassing. Minor bouts of Alzheimer's had not occurred, probably the panic of shifting out had kept it at bay, by some strange logic. He slipped out after lunch two days after the packing had started on a Wednesday while the house was taking a much-needed afternoon siesta. The people from the movers and packers agency were sprawled in the living room after a lunch of *dal, chawal, kadhi* Bhagya had prepared – the maids had already been stopped from the first of that month. Raghav was in the study immersed in sorting his papers, Bhagya and Rahul were in their room, the door was closed as the airconditioner was on. He was expected to be in his room, even though he did not use the airconditioner, he generally kept his door closed, so no one would suspect anything. Unless well after, when it was too late to do anything. He stepped out into the brilliant sunshine – it blinded his eyes – it felt somewhat like the whiteness that blinded him when all memory blanked out. He did not feel the heat, somehow it felt liberating. It warmed his bones which felt chilled to the core nowadays. The sidewalks were paved and clean, with bougainvillea spilling out over the fences of the neighbouring bungalows. He could walk along freely with no fear of running into any vehicles. Of course when the snow whiteness of the receding memory blanketed his consciousness, he would not know if he strayed onto the main road. But by then there would be the pleasant numbness of not knowing anything, until it was too late. There was a song in his head, and his heart. Freed from the confines of the house, he didn't even miss the balcony. He was free from the burden of consciously making the decision to live, or even not to live, nature would decide for him.

Raghav found him after five days when in response to his FIR, the police intimated him about an unclaimed body in the far corner of the city's downtown, the reason of death was put as brain haemorrhage due to tripping over an electric pole. As he wrapped his father's soiled, smelly body in a clean sheet and brought him home, Raghav thought he saw the faint hint of a smile on his face, the kind of smile that he had not seen on him since his mother died.

THE INTELLECTUAL

The dry grass bristled against a breeze that was grainy to the skin. All around him, as far as eye could see, were fields. But it wasn't the juicy, wavy green fields that they showed one in Bollywood movies. The land was arid, interspersed with patchy segments of paddy sown by the farmers. There was a small canal used for irrigation whenever it allowed to do so, right now a rivulet ran in it, some small children played in its muddy banks. He sat on the verandah of the house challenging the hot wind to drive him in. The insides of the house would be cool, his grandfather had built it in his time, with the stone cold floors and high rafters that ensured natural air conditioning throughout the year. But he did not want to go in, not yet. He was waiting for her. In some time, she would come walking through the fields, cutting a path across directly to the house, her multi-hued cotton *saree* making her stand out like a bright spot of colour against the colourless landscape. When she would see him, she would smile that typical half-smile of hers, he would smile in return, and together they would go in. Even a month back if someone had told him that he would be waiting in his village house on a Monday forenoon, for a woman who had never seen the archway of a college, he would have thought them mad.

The clink of glasses sounded through the open door of Vivek's library. The thick wood-panelled walls had shelves of books that spanned the entire length and breadth of English Literature. Vivek taught Literature at the University. He would often joke saying 'you know more of Shelley and Keats than me, what are you doing teaching Philosophy!' The joke often played out in his mind later, not the first part, but the second part. What indeed was he doing, teaching Philosophy. Of late it had started making still lesser and lesser sense to him. The obfuscating complexities of *Meno* or *Republic* which had been such an adrenaline kick for the grey cells when he started his job at the University, now seemed to echo off the large classroom walls, colliding with each other and falling to the ground in a heap. To be honest, the students were as attentive as their previous batches, even more so perhaps, because what he had started lacking in conviction, he made up by sheer competence accrued from years of teaching the same matter. His faculty ratings were as high as ever. But the ball dropped when it came to him, how he felt. Looking at the students staring at him, mouth agape, eyes slightly dilated, he wondered what would happen if for a moment he stopped spouting forms and ideas and asked them what use would the Socrateses and Aristotles of the world serve them. Or if he told them he felt the janitor in his view did much more valuable work than he did. He knew these were only random thoughts that helped lift his mood from time to time, he was not one of those mavericks who had the courage to actually do something radical. But he could not shake off the feeling of oppression. Not long ago he used to enjoy the shady green avenues of the University campus, the cafes and eat-outs dotting the area, the casual encounters with fellow colleagues as he took his routine morning walk. Now he felt as if all these were elements of the glass-house he occupied, a fragile, unnatural ecosystem, far removed from the realities that beset the average member of humanity. One night he had a strange dream. In the dream he was the proverbial goldfish in the bowl. Outside the bowl, masses of people congregated to see him, the goldfish, glide within a space designed to look like a miniature version of the University. He felt the eyes of the hundreds of people pressed against the glass bowl stare holes through him. All he wanted to do was to jump out of the bowl. He had woken up in a cold sweat.

But it was not limited to his work and workplace alone. If that had been the case he would have dismissed it as some kind of midlife crisis. His deep sense of disjointedness with the present and his inability to see any value add in any aspect of life seemed to signal to him a deeper malaise.

As faculty members of one of the premier institutes specializing in the humanities stream in the country, they had regular campus connect programmes where faculty members of other colleges came over to discuss academic theories, engage in debates and converge over seminars. Typically, as happened in all the so-called summits and knowledge sessions, the day would be spent in semantics, and the evening would be unwind time over drinks and dinner. This was also the time for the genders to mix in a non-academic sphere and people waited for the opportunity to connect to the opposite sex. Life in the University for the single people could be quite drab, such occasions came as a breath of fresh air. Shikha was a faculty member of a nearby college in the same University. She was quite a hit with the men, he liked her also. Smart and well-dressed, she knew how to hold her own in a conversation. Enjoyed the good things in life without going overboard. Importantly she had the reputation of being a serious and diligent teacher to the students and was looked upto by others in the campus. She and he had hit it off quite successfully in the first meeting. Thereafter whenever there was a connect programme in either his college or hers, they sought out each other imperceptibly. He began to enjoy her company more and more. Of course he had enough of his share of overtures from the fairer sex within the teaching community in that part of the world. His age ticked off all the right boxes of manliness and boyishness which apparently was the most alluring age as far as women were concerned, his was not the chiselled but craggy sort of good looks, and the fact that he dressed well and had courteous yet ruggedly simple manners only added to his *mojo*. His encounters had been brief but pleasurable, he had to admit. The women, few but impressive, that he had relationships with, gave of themselves freely, not expecting anything more than a healthy, enjoyable experience, which was pretty much what he expected too. If they had any aspirations of a lasting relation, they were smart enough not to talk about it. He kept it that way. Lately though he had begun to ask himself if it was not time enough to settle into something more permanent. Not that he craved the solidity of a permanent relationship, or he was fatigued with the evanescence of his fleeting affairs, but more so because it became irritating to ward off friends on when he would finally settle down. That, and also because the evenings sometimes became boring. Shikha could be an ideal choice. His alpha male friends teased him 'you get to have your cake and eat it too, not fair'.

What he did not tell them was even in the most intense relationship he had never given of himself completely to his partner. His soul remained aloof, never being touched by their refined and rehearsed movements. The layers of sophistication did not leave them completely, even in the most intimate of moments, they remained correct, both in body and soul. And so did he. The feeling of incompleteness never left him. In his daydreams, he dreamt of a partner who would bring in the wildness of the jungle, the rushing torrents of a river in spate, the smell of the first rains on earth and the dense green of the rainforests. What he got was the powdered eliteness of a hotel lobby. But he did not tell this to his friends, not even Vivek who was his closest colleague, he was not sure, even given their erudition, they would understand. Initially it was manageable, he still managed to get his share of fun, and not ask for too much. But slowly the gnawing feeling of missing something began growing on him. He started avoiding the connect programmes. And if he had to, he did not circulate. After a couple of evenings like that, Vivek noticed. 'Buddy, what's up, not feeling well'. 'Nah, just not in the mood' he dismissed it lightly. 'Ah, the problem of the blue stockinged Professor' saying so he went to meet someone; he was relieved that Vivek left it at that. He would have been at a loss to explain it, he himself was grappling with why he was behaving the way he was.

However Vivek could sense something was really amiss with him. It was a Saturday and the connect was in another college, the college where Shikha taught Political Science. They had left college early that day, Saturday was half-day, as anyway in the afternoon if at all there were classes most students were to be found in the nearby multiplex. It was an all-men group when he, Vivek and a couple of colleagues arrived in the large auditorium-like room where the discussions and subsequent dinner were planned. Shikha came in late that day, much after the academic discussions were over, and dinner was about to begin. He was hanging out with a couple of teachers from the same University making desultory talk about general stuff, when she walked in draped in an ashes of roses *saree*. Minimal jewellery – two small ear studs and a classy watch – and a no-fuss simple hairdo completed the get-up. Any ordinary man would feel attracted, without doubt. But the moment he felt other eyes turning towards him – while nothing was official about their relationship, it was common knowledge that they preferred each other's company – he felt horrified at even the allusion of any intimate relationship with her. With her or anyone in the same ilk. Claustrophobia gripped his throat and feeling choked in the room which was already redolent with the heavy smells of whiskey and cigarettes, he made a dash to the balcony which was hidden by thick drapes.

It was a no moon night, but the stars had chosen to relieve the night sky of complete darkness. He felt his eyes plunging into the inky blackness in the space between stars and travelling fast to a place of thick tropical vegetation, cool and calm in the confines of some unexplored land. Or going under the Niagara Falls, which would wash all over him, inside him, cooling him, filling the gaps that refused to give him the relief of completeness that he craved for so ardently.

'Hello there stranger' Shikha had walked in without his noticing. She must have observed him going to the balcony, most people did not know there was a balcony there.

'Hey' he rearranged his contours quickly and forced himself to be civil.

'Where are you hiding'

'Hiding? No, why do you say that'. He could not think of anything else to say.

'Oh come on, we know each other enough by now for me to know when you are avoiding and for you to know that I would know when you do so'. That was true, it was too obvious a lie to be believed. He chose the safest way out.

'Too much work, year end semester exams, extra classes and on top of that there is this paper I am writing.' The paper part was false, but she would not know.

'You need a break. Why don't you take that Bali trip you had been talking about.'

It seemed like an era back. He had been talking about taking a break and going to Bali, and it was at a point when they both had settled into a comfortable relationship of friends-headed-for-more in all probability. Implicit in that discussion

77

was the tacit understanding that she would accompany. It was quite the norm in the University for couples headed for a serious relationship to take off together without any noise. Of course some photographs of the vacation were bound to pop up sometime thanks to Facebook and others interested in following the matter, but generally it was not spoken about in public, the understanding being, as long as it's not official no one knows about it. And he had seriously considered it till about sometime back. Today the mere thought gave him shudders.

'Yes, I must think about it seriously'.

He quickly changed the topic to other mundane matters. She sensed it – by now she was familiar with his changing moods and his small eccentricities – but to her credit she played along. At such times he was thankful for her maturity. They continued discussing about the students, curricula, the political scenario, everything except themselves, until someone came out to the balcony to have a smoke. They came back to the party, and the rest of the evening passed in a blur at least for him. Shikha did not attempt to get close to him for the remaining part of the evening.

Back home, he threw off his tie in the drawing room, this was also unlike him, he was very meticulous about things being in their proper place. Now he couldn't care less. The study was his sanctuary, whatever the rigours of the day, he felt an unburdening of sorts once he got into his chair. Casually he flipped through the papers on the desk, when he saw an envelope with familiar handwriting. It was from his village postmaster, he doubled up as the caretaker of his ancestral home in the village. There was no one now in the house, his father had one brother who was settled in Africa long since, and he was his parents' only child. After the demise of his parents, for a long time the house was in a state of disuse, then he decided, if not out of a sense of filial duty at least common sense dictated that he undertake repairs. The postmaster, a long time loyalist of his family, his ancestors having served them for generations, offered to supervise the work. Since then he was the self-appointed caretaker of the house and kept in touch regularly over petty matters concerning the property. He opened the letter carefully, it must have been posted at least two weeks back and traversed through half the country, his village was in the interiors of north India and his University was on the hilly terrains of the north-east. The latest news was the last tenant having left, the house was empty, the question being whether it be put out to rent at the same rate or a higher one. Thoughtfully he had attached a photograph of the house along with the letter. He looked at it, a lonesome house standing surrounded by fields on all sides. If one looked minutely, one could make out an old-time grandfather recliner on the verandah, the ones they used to make with cane and wood, with a long leg-rest opening from under the armrest. All of a sudden he saw himself in the chair, looking back at himself questioningly. The image appeared so suddenly that he was taken aback. At the same moment the decision was made on where he would go for his vacation.

The journey to the village was quite tortuous. First he had to take a taxi to the nearest city, then a flight out to Calcutta (he could never bring himself to say Kolkata), then a train to the town nearest to his village and then finally a ride on something that was a cross between an autorickshaw and a tractor. He was dusty, bedraggled and on edge by the time he reached the village. Thankfully the loyal retainer was there to receive him as he alighted. Initial pleasantries over, they proceeded towards the house. For the first time since he started on his journey he felt that it had not been such a wrong decision after all; the house stood out, a white and wood apparition against the darkening evening skies. The postmaster had made all arrangements, the old cement floors were cleaned to a shine, the masterbed was laid with clean sheets and pillowcases, he had arranged for an old lady to come and cook, and to his famished body the simple dinner of *roti, dal, sabzi* and a local sweetmeat looked delicious. A refreshing cold bath in the old tiled bathroom and some food inside him, and all was right with the world again. He was too tired to unpack or even to do his customary bedtime reading, he just lay down on the bed and sleep overcame him immediately.

The next couple of days passed off uneventfully. He fell into a leisurely routine of late mornings, simple but wholesome home cooked food and long rambling conversations with the postmaster after he shut up for the night. It was on the third day of his stay that the postmaster made a request.

'*Sahib*, there is a girl here who buys the produce of trees – fruits of the fruit-bearing trees, bark and resin from others – and sells it to small-scale industries in and around who manufacture pickles, disposable plates and other such products. Poor thing is the single bread earner in the family, her father was struck with a paralytic attack some years back and has been in bed since then. No other siblings. She has studied till class twelve but then could not go further because the nearest college is five miles away. Since then for the past so many years she has been doing this, earning a livelihood. Work is good and pays well, but now the local produce is dwindling, some of the manufacturers are trying to eliminate the middlemen by trying to buy it directly from the farmers. She still gets work because everyone knows her, but she has been after me to buy the produce from your farms as she can get most of her requirements at one place.'

He knew he had inherited substantial land handed down from generation to generation. The land had been given on contract to some local farmers and the money which came from selling the paddy and other produce was put into a bank account he had opened in the village bank. He had arranged, despite protests from the postmaster, for a regular monthly amount to be paid out to him.

'Why do you want to involve me in all this, anyway you are the best person to handle it, why don't you talk to her and finalize'.

'No *Sahib*, it will be good if you can set the initial rates, the produce from the farm is quite high. After that I will supervise the payments etc.'

It made sense.

'Ok, ask her to meet me tomorrow.'

She did not come for the next two days. On the third day, spread out on the recliner, he was half-seriously reading a book on the verandah, when a spot of colour appeared in the distance. He watched curiously as the speck grew larger. It was a lady, could be in her late twenties or early thirties, dressed in a simple cotton *saree* and a printed blouse. She did not have the usual swinging gait commonly seen in women in the rural areas, rather there was a spring in her step. And something told him, though he could not see her face, that she would be smiling a half-smile. As she came closer, the pearly whites of her teeth peeping out within upturned lips, he had a chance to look at her more closely. She had the robust contours that was natural to women who worked hard and ate without the self-imposed constrictions of diet. She was of slightly dusky complexion, the one he preferred to the porcelain whiteness which felt suffocating for him. He was aware that he was staring at her as she approached near, but he could not make the superficial movement of going back to his book.

She greeted him in the traditional form. He heard himself making usual queries of family, education, how she came about doing the particular job, conscious of a playful insouciance with which she answered. Sitting on the floor of the verandah, she answered all that he asked, smiling that half smile which he had imagined when he first saw her walking in. After years, he felt an imperceptible quickening in his blood. He was surprised at himself, on no count could he think of a reason why he would be attracted to her. But it was there, unmistakable. They spoke about the business, she quoted some figures, he vaguely remembered his nodding assent, not caring to check with the postmaster if the figures quoted made sense. He was aware of her departure, when the floor in front of him suddenly lost its warmth. A long sigh escaped him involuntarily as he settled back in the recliner, he felt like a boy again.

She came again after two days, and then after a day, to formalize the deal. Meanwhile the postmaster had pulled him up gently for agreeing to what he said were rock bottom prices. He couldn't care less.

'She needs the money, it's okay' he was convincing himself as much as the retainer.

That day she came as the evening sun was dissolving in the light brown dusk. The sky promised to be overcast in some time, with the beginnings of ominous clouds gathering in the far east. The heavy restlessness of the weather began to envelop him as well. He kept pacing up and down the verandah unable to sit and do anything. He stopped when he saw the familiar colourful speck in the distance slowly coming closer. Today she was not smiling for some reason. Her forehead was adorned in a large black *bindi*, and the *saree* in white, black and red was offset with a worsted-red coloured blouse with black piping. Just as she entered the awning of the verandah, the sky came down with a vengeance, pouring out its restiveness in torrents. As he led her inside the house, he knew it was his own restiveness that was also seeking to let go.

It was the dark green of the Amazon rainforests, the cold downpour of hidden waterfalls in unexplored places, the heat of the desert sun, all come together for the next hour. There were no frills or fragrances, no refinements, no holding back lest one repel the partner, no niceties, he had never experienced anything close to it. The closest he had come was during his first initiation into the adult world, both he and the girl were inexperienced and it had been his first brush with uninhibitedness. First and also the last. Thereafter it had only been a succession of plateaus of varying undulations.

She had come almost daily after that. If a day would pass by without her coming he would send for her under some pretext. Some days they would simply sit on the verandah and chat, he in the recliner and she on the floor at his feet. She would talk about her business, how the product manufacturers tried to cheat her, good deals that she cut at times; he would talk about his work at the University not knowing how much she understood, not caring also, as long as she sat there and nodded her head. Other days they would go into the large room which had his grandfather's old rosewood bed laid out with clean cotton bedspread of local make. If the postmaster took exception to the new trend, he never said it, he just stopped coming unless called for.

As his vacation timeline came close, he sent a letter to the University asking for a sabbatical of indefinite period. There was a flurry of calls from the Dean, colleagues, Vivek, Shikha; after he tired of not answering calls, he switched off his mobile. He really had no one else who would call.

She came, like always, like a speck of color against the arid land that slowly grew bigger. The *bindi* was green today, the mood would be playful. She came in flushed from the sun, the dusky turning into a sunburnt brown. There was no need for words, as she sat down on the floor near his chair.

Pramodini

The crack in the wall was there as long as she could remember. It irritated her. It was not as if that was the only flaw in the house, in fact that was the least of the visible signs of decay. The roof was leaking in multiple places, during monsoons the house became a small playground of puddles. The plaster was peeling in places. Where it was not, the paint had become so faded that it was difficult to figure out which colour it had been originally. The only thing which annoyed her more than the crack was the calendar fluttering against the wall. He insisted on hanging it at the same place, every year, said he found it easy to read. At that spot, the fan kept on flapping it and it kept getting on her nerves. Things that had taken on a larger meaning earlier, things she had romanticized about – the steady stream of all kinds of people coming in to discuss politics, literature and hegemony of the Western world, the propaganda pamphlets exhorting the masses to stand up for their rights, the *sabhas* with the villagers – seemed empty and meaningless, even superficial. She realized it was more her frustration than anything else, she felt tied down with the weight of a decision taken eight years back, and the consequences of the decision that had played out in the intervening years. A daily battle to make ends meet with two kids and a husband who was steeped in ideology but whose *mojo* had unfortunately withered away for her at least.

It had not been like this always. When they had met first, she was in awe of his intellectual prowess, the fiery poems he used to write, his vision to change the world, all had excited and impressed her. He used to visit their house to confer with her father who had been an armchair politician. People from various walks of life used to congregate in their house. Over hot tea and *pakodas* the whole world in its various nuances would get discussed. Her job was to serve the snacks and the tea, but she used to loiter around listening to the ideas and the ideologues. Most of them were post their prime, younger than her father, but over the hill. One afternoon however, her afternoon nap was broken by a young and energetic voice reciting a poem written with the fervour of patriotism, and as she got up hurriedly and peeped through the red and white checked curtains, she saw a young man, dressed in a *khadi dhoti-kurta* sitting cross-legged near her father. He was new, but from their conversation she could make out that they were long since known to each other, meeting after a long hiatus. Quickly she rushed to engage in her assigned chores. Waking up the cook who was sprawled like a felled banyan tree in the kitchen, she kept the cups and saucers ready on a plastic serving tray. Meanwhile the cook started preparing some hot raw-banana *bhajiyas* and put the water to boil for tea. In some time she was ready with the tray laden with snacks and an aluminium kettle full of tea with cups and saucers stacked gingerly. As she served the food and tea to all those seated under the asbestos verandah, she kept glancing at him through the corner of her eye. Long-time friends of her father, who visited frequently called out to her asking which class she was in and how she was planning to spend her vacations. He was not even aware of her presence, not even when she kept the plate of *bhajiyas* and the tea in front of him. He kept rummaging through a dog-eared single-line notebook in which some scribblings seemed to look like verses penned down in black ink.

'Let me recite this one for you, have written this last week only' he was telling her father as she quietly slunk away feeling dejected and overlooked.

The next meeting was more fortuitous. She was cycling in the lane in front of their house in the afternoon one day, when she suddenly saw him walking down towards their house. In her nervousness and eagerness, she lost balance and fell down. Her knee struck the concrete floor and she could not escape a cry of pain. He rushed towards her solicitously, and helped her limp back to the house, balancing the cycle with one hand and her with the other. Her mother applied some tincture and bandages to the wound, parallely complaining to him about her wayward and whimsical ways. She looked up at him to see him very quietly smiling at her with a twinkle in his eyes. She smiled back and a deal was struck imperceptibly between them.

That signalled the start of a very unusual relationship. He was a well-known activist, sympathizer of the masses, known for his fiery verse, for being anti-establishment and an iconoclast. Well into his late thirties, nobody ever expected him to marry or settle down. As part of his sojourns he came to meet her father regularly, her father being a great admirer of his poetry, and they chatted on everything under the sun starting from the sad state of the country's political affairs, to the failure of the pro-poor schemes, what was actually needed to empower the rural denizens, literature and social issues. Into the discussions would creep in the Lenins, Stalins and Gandhis of the world too. While there would be a regular set of her father's friends – he called them Comrades – she always managed to garner a corner seat under the pretext of serving tea or snacks. Truth be said, she was awestruck by the very nature of discussions that went on, they painted the world in charmed colours of varying shades of idealism. Into this image, without her realization, crept in his visage becoming a part of the vignette. Sometimes he would linger on after the others had left. In between their conversation when her father went inside the house for something, they would strike up a conversation. Mostly she had questions around his poetry, what certain verses meant, and he would explain to her his state of mind when he wrote it, what it was meant to convey and how it got interpreted by the readers. Slowly he started coming earlier than the others, just to get some time to talk to her. Their topics started diverging into other subjects, she was in her higher secondary and literature was her subject of specialization. He quizzed her on her favourite plays and poems and she got him to check and assess her notes. On hindsight, he would have been attracted to her innocent awkwardness, her interest in areas which belied her age, and certainly her nubile charm. For some months this went on undeterred as no one suspected anything other than pure academic interest between them, the age difference being what it was. But with a woman's intuition, her mother started noticing his all-too-frequent trips especially during times when her father was bound not to be around. She admonished her and asked her father to speak to the gentleman. He stopped coming to the house but it was too late, they had reached a point of no return. They started meeting outside, on the sidelines of *sabhas* he attended, party meetings and then at his home. He had rented a small place in the city and stayed alone. She liked the sparse cleanliness of the room, the coarse cotton *chaddar* on the bed, the small wooden table with its glass of water and a half-rusty but clean and functional table lamp. It signified all that he stood for and advocated. Finally things got out of hand as people who saw them together came and reported it to her parents. On a fateful Sunday afternoon he was called to the house and her parents and some close relatives who had been called specifically for the matter, sat in a circle around him, throwing a volley of questions and intermittently castigating him for what they called cradle snatching. She was impressed with the calmness with which he handled it all, quietly replying, not being tempted to strike back at their barbs and not even once hinting at her culpability in the whole affair. There had never been any doubt in her mind but if she was seeking reaffirmation of her choice, she got it that day.

They finally decided that they would give them both six months to change their minds and separate, if it didn't happen, then they would know what steps to take. It was an excruciating six months. Her higher secondary final exams were approaching so she had to stick to her books leaving her little opportunity to go out of the house. He did not come to their house again strictly following the terms of agreement. The only way of getting in touch with each other was through letters and that was also strictly monitored by her parents. Postal missives was out of the question, it was only through friends and acquaintances that they kept in touch.

Somehow the six months had come to an end. Her parents had expected the whole episode to blow over, not expecting what they thought to be puppy love, to survive opprobrium, forced separation and societal rigour; they found themselves sadly mistaken. What made things more difficult was that she did not do too well in her exams. Of course she passed, but her scores were way below what was expected out of her as she had always been an exemplary student. Her peers secured positions in the State list of toppers and went on to crack entrance exams to various professional courses, she neither did too well in the academic side nor could she secure admission to any specialized courses. A family meeting was called urgently. Opinion was undivided, he had been responsible for her debacle in the exams, there was no way in any case that they could be together, they were divided by multiple things but most of all by age. As she quietly stood behind the sitting room curtains and despaired of any future together, suddenly her father spoke up. He looked very old and tired, as if he was weighed down with the burden of something he could not fight any longer.

'Let her marry him. We have given them time to change their minds. That has not happened. On top of that, she has lost interest in studies, the career we had dreamt about for her will probably never happen. Then what's the whole point of holding back. Let her be happy at least'.

Each word sliced her heart like a knife. She had let them down, in every way possible. More so, she had let herself down, she could feel it deep down in her bones. Her dreams and her reality were too far removed from each other.

The family had erupted in disbelief and outrage at her father's suggestion. But he stood his ground with a quiet steadfastness and finally prevailed. He was called to the house, the verdict was passed, possible marriage dates were discussed and fixed a month from then. Would any of his relatives attend? No, he had lost his parents early, and had no close relatives in touch. A distant uncle or two would attend, but that was it. In fact that had been another nail in the coffin, a person with no known family ties was not someone you could entrust your daughter to. For her the month passed in a blur. She seemed to see everything in slow motion, like an outside spectator – her mother stolidly going about clothes and other things she would need to take with her with no trace of the nervous excitement one would expect in such a situation, her father giving instructions to the caterer, the decorators and other vendors quietly with a note of resignation in his voice, other relatives giving quizzical looks to her as they went about sundry chores. Only her young cousins engaged in the usual gossip and banter and teased her about the upcoming nuptials. But instead of feeling excited or apprehensive it only served to irritate her. She had an inexorable feeling of hurtling towards a future which she designed for herself quite inadvertently.

The marriage and her departure from the house happened, for her at least, in a similar blur where she felt she was going through the motions, playacting for the benefit of others. The reality sunk in when she alighted from the car to step into her new house. It was done up prettily in marigold flowers, inside the house all the chairs had cushions in colourful cotton covers, the tables and bed had been covered with vibrant handloom covers and the whole house had a festive air about it. An aunt, the wife of the distantly related uncle has been instrumental in it. She felt deeply grateful to her. After the initial few days of rituals and festivities, the handful of relatives and friends who had come down for the wedding started to leave. She was not unhappy to see them go, she wanted some quiet and peace, the whole month had been too stressful and painful.

With a sigh she came back to the present. The initial few months had been blissful, she had to admit. Just managing to be together after the protracted period of separation was by itself a high. He had been gentle, passionate and sensitive in their intimate moments. She had felt complete.

It was difficult to pin-point when the journey of disenchantment started. After their first child he had announced to her his decision to move back into his area of activism, it was a village which took six hours by bus from where they stayed. Of course he made it sound like a consensual decision.

"We have to shift our base, a lot of work I started there has stayed unfinished. The people there need us. You will also want to be a part of the movement there and contribute your bit."

What could she say. Wasn't their whole relationship built on similar values and ideologies. Anyway the baby was small, and it did not matter where they lived, most of her time would go in tending to the baby. She agreed, not that she was really asked.

She remembered the day they shifted out. That was really the day she felt it was a *bidaai* for her. The tiny house they stayed in, had come to assume the position of home, from which she felt she was being torn away. Whatever disillusionment, disenchantments life would have handed out to her, she could have bore it in that house. Going away from the city she was born in, to some Godforsaken village to tend to the democratic ideals of her husband seemed too far removed from her own romantic ideas of a larger cause. Her last memory of the house was the blooming *champa* tree at the far end of the small courtyard they had, its leaves were aflutter in the gentle breeze that was blowing.

Cut to the present. She came back to reality with a sigh. To be honest it had not been so difficult or unbearable at the start. On hindsight that was probably because she still had the dim hope that all his efforts would amount to something tangible in the end. Joining a political party possibly. A ticket to the assembly elections. Or even to the Parliament, who knows. Or even an informal local political satrap. That and the novelty of seeing so many people come for his advice, suggestions and counselling. There would be hectic parleys late into the night, huddled over a kerosene lantern when the local power supply played truant. At her father's it had been more theoretical discussions, this was the real thing. It would shape up to something. Plus she had her hands full with the baby. She conceived again when the first born was three, and so just as she was getting out of full-time motherhood, it chose her again. She again went into the cycle of late night feedings, staying up whole nights while the infant wailed, dozing and sleep-walking through the morning chores, she shuddered to think how she bore it for a second time all over again. And she was petrified all the time of the scenario of what if she conceived again. Many-a-time she toyed with the idea of going to the nearby primary health care centre and getting sterilized. But even five years of staying in the hinterland had not fortified her to stand the horrors of the unhygienic, smelly, ten-bedded hospital with stained sheets, chipped ceramic urinals and the naked bulbs that kept on flickering throughout the night. She would die of an infection there, if not from the surgery going wrong. So she cringed and bore the fear of a third embryo within her womb.

She remembered the moment even today. It was the forenoon of some weekday, she lost count most of the times, it did not matter anyway. The elder kid was in school, she had started to go to a local nursery school, and the younger one, now two, played in the small mud-washed courtyard as she sat on the steps in a reverie. It was like an epiphany. Like someone had suddenly clicked their fingers and the halo of the last five years lifted like a smog. He would never make it, would never be someone, someone who counted somewhere. He did get invited to *sabhas* and *samitis* but now he went alone. And he read his poem and he came back. There were no tickets that he was offered, not even asked to run for the local ward elections. Politicians who sometimes visited the area, did a perfunctory *namaste* when they met him and moved on. On occasions when she accompanied him to the political rallies addressed by some visiting Minister, she would seek for some sign of recognition, some hushed conversations between them which would raise her hopes again. But none came. Sometimes she thought if they had been staying in the hills probably, in a cool place, she could have borne the rest. But the heat, and the humidity seemed to aggravate her sense of suffocation. On nights when he would be away attending some meeting or recital outside the village, the humming mosquitoes settled down on his side of the bed, occasionally leaving red marks on the skins of the children. Not that his presence was any relief, he would lie down and go to sleep almost immediately, with soft snores issuing in the darkness. She could not stand it, sometimes she felt if it was the noisy, nasal snoring most people did, she could have withstood it, the gentle snoring made her feel mad.

The end came as suddenly as she had thought. It was morning. The school had a holiday and both the kids were playing outside the house. He was talking to some people who had come with a wrangle that had happened between two local political chieftains. Why did he even care to spend time and effort on such things when what he said or did would make absolutely no difference to the matter. Anyway, she was past all that. There was a bus which left the village, for the city, at nine sharp. No one travelled on it that far, the Government plied it as a result of some pre-poll promise it had made. And no one would suspect her going anywhere other than some stops away, most villagers used it more as a ferrying medium to nearby villages. She looked back and saw the kids waving to her, she would figure out how to get them later. She did not yet know what path her freedom would take. Maybe she would get together with some rich businessman, the cracked mirror in the tin-roofed bath told her that inspite of two kids she still retained the figure of a girl. Or she would just get a job, be free and on her own, and make ends meet with struggle but with joy. There was time to deal with it. For now, she would let the morning breeze from the window of the bus play with her hair, and let the burden fall away.

Printed in the United States
By Bookmasters